THE SERVANT AND MISTRESS STORIES

The Servant and Mistress Stories

THAMES RIVER PRESS
An imprint of Wimbledon Publishing Company Limited (WPC)
Another imprint of WPC is Anthem Press (www.anthempress.com)
First published in the United Kingdom in 2013 by
THAMES RIVER PRESS
75–76 Blackfriars Road
London SE1 8HA

www.thamesriverpress.com

A CIP record for this book is available from the British Library.

ISBN 978-0-85728-135-7

This title is also available as an eBook

THE SERVANT AND MISTRESS STORIES

LUCINDA RHYS–EVANS

THAMES RIVER PRESS

Foreword

On the basis of documentation found after his death, I have adapted and edited the erotic stories that the writer and academic Stephen Mason drafted between January and July 2001 and print them here in – as far as can be ascertained – the order they were written.

The Burning Cockpit, She and Me, The Fundraiser (written after his experience at the Hong Kong Institute of the Arts Gala Ball), *The Terrorists* and *The Riders* are more complex in terms of characterization, while the first three tales – along with *The Framing* and *Mademoiselle Camille* – concentrate primarily on the writer's physical predilections. We know the author acted out three of the stories (*The Dinner Invitation, Mademosielle Camille* and *The Riders*) and that two (*The Interview* and *The Cleaner*) were inspired by figures in his domestic and work environments.

Of the ten stories, seven are told in the first person, three in the third, seven from a male and three from a female perspective. All the stories are self-contained entities and have no narrative connection with one another, or any direct connection with the life of the author as described in my book *Servant and Mistress* – though there are several overlaps and parallels with his real, as opposed to imagined, sexual activity. What does bind the stories together is setting: apart from the last one (*The Riders*), they all take place in Hong Kong.

Finally, if you are reading the stories first, without knowing anything about their author or the unusual context in which they were written, I hope you will want to find out more. I hope their strangeness, their erotic and sometimes pornographic excess will make you curious about the person who wrote them – all within six months of his death – and encourage you to read the companion volume mentioned above.

Lucinda Rhys-Evans

THE DINNER INVITATION

She rang me one afternoon at the office, around three o'clock. I was staring out of the window, watching a Star Ferry bob up and down in the wake of an express catamaran to Discovery Bay. I was also trying to balance an un-balanceable budget for the Music School – of which, for my sins, I am Dean – and her interruption was welcome.

"Hello, Robert. Angel here. Do you remember me?"

"Yes," I said after a moment's pause for reflection. "You were at Karin's party."

"That's right. I was the one you talked to about healthy eating."

I laughed.

"Yes. I'm sorry. Did I bore you?"

"On the contrary. You inspired me."

Her voice sounded more forceful than I remembered, more authoritative. I had met her two or three weeks ago at a party at my Dutch friend Karin's flat on Mount Butler Road. And I did remember her. She was Chinese, five foot two, long black hair and not immediately noticeable. But then neither was I, and she had noticed me.

"As a result of our conversation, I'd like to invite you to dinner, next Tuesday," she continued. "Can you come?"

I tapped a key and called up my on-screen diary.

"Yes," I said, after scanning the information in front of me. "Why not?"

I had a resources meeting earlier that evening, but I was the boss and it could be kept short.

"I live at Old Peak Road, No. 18," she said. "28th floor. Flat A. The porter will ring up when you arrive."

Her Chinese accent was not pronounced, but made her English sound official, as if she were summoning me. Too many government directives, I thought. All Hong Kongers have been taught to speak English like civil servants.

"Fine. What time?"

"Seven thirty?"

"Can we make it eight?"

"Of course. Oh, and one more thing."

"Yes?"

The Star Ferry had docked at Tsim Tsa Tsui and my eyes were now following a PLA helicopter that had taken off from Tamar.

"Could you wear a dinner jacket?"

I laughed.

"Is the Chief Secretary on your guest list?"

"No. There are no other guests. It's just, well, I like to dress up for dinner."

"All right," I said. "See you Tuesday."

"Thank you, Robert. I shall look forward to it."

I hadn't used my DJ since last year's graduation dinner, but at least I had one.

I rang Karin and asked what she knew about Angel. Not much. She was an investment banker in Central, and renowned for her culinary skills. Her meals were always described as 'out of this world,' but no specific details of the menu were ever given. All guests were sworn to secrecy.

"Someone must have told?" I said.

"No. No one. If they do, they're not invited back. And everyone wants to be."

"The food must be good."

"Yes."

"Have you ever been?" I asked.

"No," said Karin. "I'm not a man."

"She only asks men?"

"So I've heard."

Karin had to go, and hung up. I returned to surveying Victoria Harbour, my chances of balancing the budget remoter than ever. I had been hand-picked to eat with an Angel, whose secrets could never be told. What more could a man want?

The following Tuesday, I curtailed discussion of money for a new grand piano, implied that anyone with any other business would be fired and headed for home.

I showered, put on clean underwear and a newly pressed dress shirt, dug out my dinner jacket, peeled off the dry cleaner's polythene and was soon looking like Pierce Brosnan without the muscles. I clipped on a bow tie, having long ago forgotten how to tie one, grabbed a bottle of Chateau D'Arcins from a rack in the kitchen and headed out into the humid air of Happy Valley to hail a taxi.

Fifteen freezing minutes later – the vehicle's air-con must have been set at 10°C – the driver announced our arrival at '*Gau San Deng Do Sabaho.*' I glanced out and saw the number '18' embossed in gold on the wall of a marble-clad high-rise block.

"Thanks," I said, handing across a larger tip than usual.

The porter, an unctuous little man in a navy blue uniform, announced my arrival and saw me to the lift with much smiling and nodding. Hoping for a late *Lai See*, no doubt, it was only two weeks since Chinese New Year and the season for handing out little red packets with money inside was still in full swing.

On the way up to the 28th floor, I checked my appearance. Short-cut red hair with grey flecks discreetly dyed, face attractively wrinkled, stomach firm. Not bad for a fifty-year-old and well within the category 'interesting.'

When I emerged, she was waiting.

She shook my hand and led me down a carpeted corridor into a tastefully furnished living room with a panoramic view across Central and Eastern Districts to the hills of Lantau beyond. I glanced at the vista and then turned my attention to her.

Long black hair swept off a high forehead by a Thai silk band; a fine-boned face with discreet makeup and dark eyes; fifties-style, peach satin cocktail dress cut high to the neck and low to the knee, with flared skirt and bodice top encasing a slim, well-proportioned body; fine-meshed, flesh-coloured silk stockings descending into immaculately crafted, beige leather shoes with sharp-pointed toes and high heels. A demure yet commanding presence, that promised civilised conversation and pleasant companionship for the evening ahead – a dinner hostess from yesteryear: polite, considerate, attractive and intelligent. I was glad she had asked me to wear a dinner suit.

I handed over my offering of wine and she carried it to the kitchen. I glanced at the table and noticed it was laid for one. She returned with a tray of drinks and saw the direction of my gaze.

"Please, Robert," she said, indicating a chintz sofa. "Take a seat. Then I will explain how my dinner parties work. A drink, perhaps?"

"Yes. Thank you. Scotch, please. Straight with no ice."

I sat down and waited.

She poured a measure of whisky and a mineral water for herself. She set my glass down on a mahogany side table by the sofa and sank gracefully into an armchair opposite. She smiled and crossed her legs, smoothing the satin of her skirt over her knee.

"To a pleasant evening, Robert," she said, raising her glass.

"Yes. Indeed."

I sipped the whisky and felt the smoothness of a single-malt touch my tongue.

"Glenlivet," she said, without prompting. "I hope you like it."

"Perfect, Angel."

I smiled and noticed she was observing me with an almost disconcerting intensity.

"Robert," she said, uncrossing her legs and sitting forward. "As my guest, you have a choice. You may opt for a meal ordered from an excellent *traiteur* in Hollywood Road – his menu is on the table beside you and the food will be perfectly prepared and delivered within half an hour – or you may opt for my speciality."

"Well, obviously…" I began, but she held up her hand.

"Before you decide, I must tell you that if you opt for my dish there are certain conditions attached."

"Conditions?" I said, raising my eyebrows and taking another sip of whisky.

"A ritual is involved," she continued. "Perhaps that is a better way of putting it."

I nodded, curious to know more. Previous dinner guests would hardly have sealed their lips for a high-class takeaway – however fine the food. Of that, I was sure.

"Point one: I eat first," she explained. "That way I can give you my full attention and ensure complete satisfaction when you are served your food."

"An original approach," I said, a twinkle in my eye.

"Yes." Her tone remained serious, her gaze fixed on my face. "Point two: While I eat, you act as my servant."

I laughed and took a gulp of whisky.

"The perfect waiter? Sounds fun."

"Yes," she said again, a hint of a smile playing across her lips. "In a manner of speaking. But, if you disobey or mock my orders, you forfeit your right to the surprise dish. Home delivery will then still be on offer. What do you say?"

I drained my glass and set it down on a walnut table next to the sofa.

"I'm game," I replied. "I was a waiter in my youth. 'Madam this,' 'Madam that,' I know the drill."

"You will call me Ma'am, not Madam."

I shrugged my shoulders and rose from my seat. She waved me back.

"Dinner will be served in half an hour. Until then you are still Robert, my honoured guest. When I say it is time to eat, you will remove your jacket and stand at the head of the table. From that moment on, I shall call you 'Boy.' Is that understood?"

"Yes, Ma'am."

For the first time that evening, she laughed – her face relaxing, her eyes gleaming in the twilight, as if she had won some kind of victory.

We chatted for the next half hour and only once or twice did my thoughts – or my stomach – turn to the mystery meal ahead. She asked me about my work and told me about her job as a broker. We talked about politics and culture. I said I found Hong Kong a stimulating place, though sometimes a little philistine. She agreed.

She preferred London for the arts, but missed the energy of Hong Kong when in Europe. She enjoyed going to concerts and was fond of opera. My favourite too, I said, and we were just getting into an involved discussion about the relative merits of Verdi and Puccini when she stood up, walked to the window and turned her back towards me.

I had been in mid-sentence and felt offended by her abrupt change of mood.

"Boy," she said in a new, harsh voice. "Go to your place."

My first reaction was to rebel, to ignore her command. Then I remembered her warning and her conditions for tasting the speciality. I stood up and felt a little dizzy.

"Hurry up," she snapped. "I don't like dinner to be late."

I grinned sheepishly and removed my jacket.

"And when I speak to you, say, 'Yes ma'am!'" she added, closing a set of curtains and turning on hidden down-lighters that lit the room like a stage set. "Understood?"

"Yes, ma'am!"

I glanced at the kitchen door and wondered about the food. No smell or sound of cooking. Was she expecting me to do the honours? Was that the surprise? Prepare your own meal? No, that would not be a secret worth keeping either. I straightened my bowtie and positioned myself at the table. A footstool stood on the floor next to the single dining chair, beside that a wastepaper basket.

She glided across the room, her satin dress swishing in the plush, down-lit silence, and sat on the chair. She cleared her throat and held up an arm.

"Napkin!"

I unfurled the white linen square and laid it across her lap.

"Would mad— ma'am like some wine…?" I began.

"Do not speak unless spoken to," she snapped. "Understood?"

"Yes, ma'am!" I said, tongue still in cheek.

She sat in silence, looking me up and down.

"Stand straight."

"Yes, ma'am."

I straightened my shoulders and held my head erect.

"Now, fetch me wine from the kitchen. The Bordeaux by the door."

I found an uncorked bottle of '89 and glanced round for any signs of cooking. There were none. The mystery dish must be hidden, so as not to spoil the surprise. My hunger increased, along with my curiosity. I returned and poured Angel a thimbleful of wine. She tasted it, swished it round her mouth and nodded. I filled her glass and placed the bottle on the table beside three bowls of crudités – celery sticks, baby carrots with leafy stalks and fingers of Japanese cucumber. A fourth bowl was filled with olive oil.

"I will try the celery," she said, without looking up.

"Yes, ma'am," I said, bowing slightly.

I placed the bowl of celery before her and returned to my position. With a practiced hand she immersed a segment in the olive oil and slipped it into her mouth. I heard the muted sound of crunching as she bit into the crisp watery flesh.

"Cucumber," she said, once the celery had been dispatched with a sip of wine.

I removed the first bowl and replaced it with a second.

Again, she dipped the vegetable in oil, sucked the flesh into her mouth and moved her jaw up and down three or four times before swallowing.

I watched and felt a pang of hunger stab my stomach. Her deliberate mastication had activated my salivary glands.

"And carrots," her voice commanded, after a dab of her lips with the napkin.

I placed the bowl of leafy-topped roots before her. This time she spent longer coating the flesh in oil and did not put it in her mouth.

"Remove your trousers!" she said, without looking up.

I almost burst out laughing. Then remembered her directive to take the ritual seriously or forfeit the mystery meal.

She watched as I slipped off my trousers, folded them and hung them over the back of a walnut chair by the door. I returned to my place. She lifted the carrot out of the oil, let the excess green fluid drain off and held it up to me.

"Hungry?"

"Yes, ma'am."

The carrot approached my mouth and stopped.

"Stand on the footstool," Angel commanded.

"Yes, ma'am."

I stood on the footstool, and parted my lips to receive the carrot.

"Turn around!"

"Yes, ma'am."

I turned, mouth still open, and felt her hands lift my shirttail and lower my underpants. My buttocks were parted and the tip of the carrot inserted into my anus – a millimetre or two, at first, and then further and further. I closed my mouth, gritted my teeth and, for a moment, rebelled. This was too much. Then rebellion turned to disgust. Was this Angel going to make me eat what she had inserted – or eat it herself?

I was on the verge of abandoning my role and demanding the Wanchai takeaway, when I heard her voice – this time soft and soothing – close to my ear.

"Painful?" she whispered.

"Yes, ma'am," I replied, though the pain was edged with unexpected arousal that diluted my disgust.

"I will stop then," she said, removing the carrot. "My last guest allowed me to insert the whole thing. He had a green tail – and a bright red face. Very fetching."

The carrot was withdrawn and dropped into the wastepaper basket. She stroked my bottom for a while and then dropped the shirttail.

"Face me."

I obeyed.

"Lift the front of your shirt."

I did as she requested and saw her eyes move to my erect penis.

A smile flickered over her lips. She reached out and enclosed the swollen member in her left hand, moving her long-nailed fingers slowly up and down its shaft. I closed my eyes and tried to think of England, but only dark-painted, Chinese lips came to mind.

"Don't move," she snapped, as I put out a hand to stroke her cheek.

She weighed my balls in her palm, squeezing them like fruit on a market stall.

I tensed.

"Don't worry. I'm not going to eat them."

She laughed, removed the napkin from her lap and stood up.

"While I go and wash my hands, I want you to fetch strawberries and cream from the fridge. Then remove the rest of your clothing and stand by my chair as before."

I did as requested, disappointed to find no sign of my special dish in the fridge.

My stomach rumbled and the erection subsided. I had no objection to sex, if that was what she wanted, but not as a *hors d'oeuvre*. I did not enjoy intercourse on an empty stomach. I removed my clothing and stood by her chair, hands across my groin.

"Please!" she remarked on her return, a hint of scorn in her voice. "No modesty."

She repositioned my hands by my side, sat down, and dipped a strawberry in the cream. She bit into it and then stared up at me, her lips red with strawberry juice.

"Hungry?"

"Yes, ma'am."

"Food soon. Don't worry."

She chuckled, scooped some cream from the bowl and spread it over the circumcised tip of my penis.

"Hold it out!"

I took the cream-covered member in my hand.

"Closer," she commanded

I stretched the semi-erect flesh towards her lips. She opened her mouth and let her tongue slide back and forth in anticipation. Then it darted forward and licked off a portion of the cream. Her nose wrinkled in disdain, her head shook in disappointment

"Too soft. I like my ice cream hard."

I blushed. She threw her napkin at me.

"Clean yourself up, and bring me a fresh glass of wine."

She stood up, crossed to the chintz sofa and lay back with her eyes closed. I wiped away the cream and pulled on my underpants.

"I know what you're doing!" she snapped. "Don't!"

"But…"

"Don't 'but' me, boy!"

"Yes, ma'am," I said, and removed the pants.

I poured a fresh glass of wine and set it down beside her. She told me to massage her forehead, but, after a minute or two, pushed my hands away.

"Lie down on the carpet, with your legs apart and feet towards me. Rest your head on a cushion and put your arms by your side."

I selected a cushion and did as she asked.

She leant forward and tucked a high-heeled shoe under my balls. Its pointed toe poked into my anus. I winced. She inserted the toe further, watching as my penis grew and throbbed beneath her gaze.

"That's better."

She rose from the sofa, walked across the carpet and stood above me – her feet positioned either side of my head, her shoes digging into my shoulders.

I found myself staring up into the canopy of her skirt, along pale stockings, past white suspenders to a pair of peach-silk cami-knickers.

She stood for a while in silence and then spoke.

"Hungry, boy?"

"Yes, ma'am."

"Want some food?"

"Yes, ma'am."

She laughed, stepped off me and returned to the sofa. She lifted up her legs, pulled off the knickers and threw them at me

"Eat those!"

I hesitated.

"Eat."

I put the knickers to my lips. They smelt of perfume, of her. She watched.

"Not hungry?"

"Yes, ma'am, but…"

She stood up, grabbed the knickers and stuffed them into my mouth.

"Then eat!"

She sat back on the sofa and watched as I sucked and chewed on the still-warm silk. Occasionally she jabbed at my erect penis with the tapering heel of her shoe, teasing the taut foreskin with skill and precision.

Again, I reached out an arm to hold her.

"Don't," she hissed, kicking my balls to add weight to her words. "Don't move."

She stood up and repositioned herself above my head.

This time I was staring up at a firm, naked behind with a glistening bush of black hair beneath. She lifted her skirt, parted the hair and passed a finger across wet lips.

"Want the main course?" she called down.

"Yes, ma'am," I whispered, my mouth muffled by the panties.

"Sure?"

Her hand played back and forth across the lips until they parted.

"Yes, ma'am," I repeated.

"Then milk yourself."

I hesitated, not sure what she meant.

Her own hand moved faster.

"I said milk yourself, boy. Take your apology for a penis and make some milk."

I felt myself blush from top to toe.

"But…" I began, her surprise dinner now less important than my self-respect.

"Do as I say," she said, bending down and stuffing the panties further into my mouth. "You don't want to be the first to fail, do you?"

I shook my head.

Was my penis an apology? Were those of her other guests larger? It felt large enough to me, and, as my fingers slid up and down, I determined to prove it could deliver.

Angel watched, and then returned to her standing position above my face. She felt for her clitoris and again began to massage it.

"Faster," she called, as her hand picked up speed.

I did my best, trying to banish the shame welling up in my empty stomach. I concentrated on her legs, her bottom, on the flick of her fingers and, at last, felt myself coming.

"Go on," she called, her voice thick with lust. "Let me see the milk!"

It came in a sharp, painful burst over my stomach, just as she climaxed above me. I felt tears in my eyes and closed them, oblivious to Angel's moans of pleasure.

After a moment, she bent down, removed the knickers from my mouth and dabbed them in the liquid on my stomach.

"Open!" she commanded.

I saw a corner of damp silk hover above my lips.

"But…" I protested.

"Open up!"

I obeyed and felt her smear my tongue and lips with gobs of the still-warm fluid.

"Taste good?"

"Yes, ma'am," I mumbled, as a second helping was scooped from my belly and forced into my mouth.

"Always tastes better," she whispered. "Food you've cooked yourself."

THE INTERVIEW

He was out of a job.

After four lucrative years at Hong Kong University, he had been given the boot. The department of languages could no longer afford to run courses in Dutch and Mr Charles Blake's contract would not be renewed after expiry in April. He had been informed three months ago, but refused to face the reality of impending unemployment. Now he had six weeks to find a job. Six weeks to find a new source of income to pay for his expensive Conduit Road apartment, his ex-family in England, and his leisured lifestyle of good meals, weekends abroad, expensive girlfriends and subscriptions to both Country and Foreign Correspondent Clubs.

He had kept half an eye on Academic Appointments in the *South China Morning Post*, but these now required knowledge of English and Chinese and, despite four years in Hong Kong, his Cantonese was limited. He could say *Josan* and *Nei ho ma*, recognize the character for 'big,' and add *la* to English words, but that was about it. Not enough to land a well-paid post with fifteen per cent gratuity at City U. And even where Chinese was not essential, there was still the problem of his age. Pushing fifty. No longer a good proposition for universities keen to save money with 'young blood' appointments.

Time to return to Europe, perhaps. But where: Holland, England, the Costa Brava? And what to do once there? Fade away on a Euro pension with a Euro wife? No way! He didn't want to exchange Wanchai for Willesden, swap young oriental bodies for a wrinkled western widow. No way! He'd be mad to leave

Hong Kong with its endless supply of Filipinos, Indonesians, Thais and *tai-tais* all happy to start relationships or have affairs despite his age and their youth. All undemanding girls keen to please, not minding if he wanted to lie back and sleep after a hard day at the Club. Happy to let him have his way, as long as they had his money – especially the *tai-tais*. They liked money and status and Charles liked them: spoilt, rich thirty-somethings from the Peak; over-whitened, jaded ladies ever on the lookout for adventure to relieve the tedium of their marriage goldmines, charity bashes and endless shopping sprees.

So he began studying the vacancies with diligence and, one morning at work, during the first of several coffee breaks, saw the following advertisement:

Wanted: Distinguished English gentleman aged 45–50 to act as Hospitality Manager for successful international firm. Good looks, good manners, willingness to please and ability to socialize most important requirements. Phone 2831 4670.

He was about to turn the page when a figure at the end of the text caught his eye: *Salary $150,000HK per month*. Good money, more than he was earning at HKU, and more than enough to keep nubile Thais and *tai-tais* turned on by his Midas touch.

He dialled the number.

"Hello, Asian International Trading," said a well-spoken English voice with the hint of an Indian accent. "How can I help?"

"I'm ringing about the job..."

"10 a.m. tomorrow. 16th floor, Chung Kai Bank building, Stubbs Road."

"I wanted to..."

"Name?"

"Blake. Charles Blake."

"Fax a CV and be here at ten. In a suit and tie, please."

"Yes, of course, and your name is...?"

But she had gone.

Charles stared out of his window at a 747 jetting off to some exotic location. He needed money. He would go. He drained his coffee, printed a CV and placed it in the fax machine beside his desk. He pressed 'send' and watched his life disappear down the line.

The next morning, a thick South China Sea mist hung over the mountains behind his flat, infusing the air with a bone-chilling dampness. Charles dug out a grey, Pierre Cardin worsted suit with a double-vented jacket. It was dated, but gave him a distinguished air and would keep out the cold. He selected a cream shirt with a faint stripe and chose a dark blue, English club tie to emphasise his credentials as a gentleman. He hailed a taxi and gave the address.

It was only a short ride by way of Kennedy Road and, as they turned up past the Sikh Temple at the foot of Stubbs Road, the Chung Kai Bank building loomed out of the mist. Next door lay a British military cemetery for the deceased victims of a nineteen-twenties cholera epidemic, and to keep these sick spirits of a colonial past at bay, or make them more at home, the bank building had – in the name of good *feng shui* – fitted coffin-shaped windows on every floor.

Charles paid the taxi, entered the bank and ascended to the sixteenth floor.

A marble-floored corridor offered him a choice of four doors, all with the name 'Asian International Trading' embossed in gold. He chose one furthest from the lift and pressed a buzzer. The door was opened by a woman in a black suit with padded shoulders and a crisp white blouse buttoned to the neck. She was tall, had long black hair and the face of a Spanish flamenco dancer – flared nostrils, a cruel curl to the lips and hard eyes.

"Come in, Mr Blake," she said. "I'm Satya Ranjit."

She indicated a wicker chair beside a glass-topped table.

"Please, take a seat."

Charles sat down and surveyed his surroundings.

The space was more like a living room than an office: leather sofas, a coffee table with magazines, a state of the art AV centre and two standard lamps with wicker shades.

He watched Ms Ranjit move to a swivel chair behind the table.

To match her tailored suit she was wearing black tights and black high heels. Power dressed in the manner of an eighties businesswoman. And that made sense. She was, he guessed, a thirty-something with tastes and temperament fine-tuned in the decade of upwardly mobile brokers and man-eating material girls.

"Mr Blake," she said. "Your CV states that you lived in Holland?"

He turned his attention from legs to face. Not bad in both departments. The Indian lilt was attractive, too. An affair with the new boss might well be on the agenda.

"Yes," he said, fixing his most charming smile in place. "I worked at the University of Amsterdam, after my spell at Cambridge. Interesting experience."

"You speak Dutch?"

"Yes. Fluently."

She nodded and flipped over the pages of his CV on the table in front of her.

"That could be useful. We have one or two clients from Holland."

She replaced the three sheets of paper in a plastic folder.

"That all seems to be in order."

She sat back in the high-backed leather chair, folding her arms as she did so.

"Mr Blake, this is an extremely important job. A job with specific duties and responsibilities, for which, I may add, we pay well."

He nodded and felt himself relax. He was going to walk this.

"The post-holder will be expected to cater to the needs and wishes of our clients, and be amenable and responsive to any requests for entertainment they may make."

"What is the nature of your business?" Charles asked.

"Import and export. Clothing mostly."

"And your clients – from all over? Men of the world, so to speak?"

"Yes, Mr Blake – from all over, but not men. Only women."

Charles raised an eyebrow and smiled.

"Very progressive, if I may say so."

"Yes. In a manner of speaking."

She stood up and walked behind him.

"Mr Blake, in this interview I will test your ability to respond to certain social situations. You have the right to stop me at any point in the process, but… "

Charles smiled again, this time more to himself. Fresh from a seminar on interview techniques by the sound of it – he recognised the language, knew the drill.

"I understand," he said.

"…but," she continued, "if you do not cooperate with our tests, you may lessen your chances of employment."

He nodded. She was being straight. Do what she asked, and do it well, and he would be home and dry – his Hong Kong lifestyle bankrolled and back on track.

"Do you agree to these terms?"

"Of course. I want the job."

"Good."

She returned to her seat, settled back in the soft leather and narrowed her eyes.

"As I said, Mr Blake, our company's clients are women, some as young as thirty, some in their sixties. But all successful businesswomen who like to relax and have fun."

"Of course," he said again.

"This morning, I am going to pretend to be one of these women. An older woman on a short visit to our office to finalise a deal – a woman with a variety of needs and whims, a woman who finds a well-groomed, mature English gentleman entirely at her service. I want to see how well you respond to her changing moods, how deftly you handle the differing demands she may make on you."

"As hospitality manager?"

"Yes, Mr Blake, as hospitality manager."

"Fire away!"

He liked role-playing interviews.

"One last point, Mr Blake – before I begin. You will always call me 'Ms Ranjit,' and only speak when spoken to. The clients prefer it that way."

"Yes, Ms Ranjit," he said, settling more comfortably into his seat.

"I will call you 'Blake.'"

He was about to suggest that Charles might be more appropriate when she spoke again.

"Stand up and show me your penis, Blake."

He felt himself redden.

"I'm sorry?"

"I've spent a day with bankers, Blake, and I'm bored. Open your flies and take your penis out. I want to see how it compares to my husband's."

He thought of the $150,000 and took a deep breath.

"Yes, Ms Ranjit."

He stood up, unbuttoned his flies and reached inside. His penis was fast asleep. He manoeuvred it into the open and let it hang against his suit trousers. He felt a fool.

She stared at the morsel of flesh, reached out her dark, nail-varnished fingers and yanked it across the table, stretching the limp protuberance to its maximum length. She then measured it against a wooden ruler and flicked it away with the back of her hand.

"My husband's is twice the size."

She wiped her hand on a tissue and leant back in the leather chair.

Charles stood, penis dangling, not sure what to do.

"Put it away, Blake. And get me an orange juice. From the tray by the television."

Relieved that the first test was past, he tucked his penis back in his pants and fetched the drink. He placed it on the table and sat down.

"Only sit when I tell you to, Blake," she snapped.

He wasn't used to being ordered around by women, but he stood up.

She sipped the drink, uncrossing her legs as she did so.

"Remove your trousers and kneel under the table."

Turning red as a Chinese flag, he, again, did as she asked.

She swung the chair round on its base, until her knees touched his nose.

"Place your head between my legs."

She opened her legs and he pushed his head up under her skirt. She was wearing stockings and suspenders, not tights. All black. She tightened her thighs around his ears, pressed her crotch against his balding head and moved it in a circular motion.

"I'm wearing silk panties, Blake. Bought in Paris. Would you like to lick them?"

Charles mumbled something into the leather seat of the chair.

The legs squeezed harder.

"I can't hear, Blake."

"If you wish, Ms Ranjit."

"Lick then. The panties, not me."

Charles raised his head and saw black silk stretched taught in front of his eyes. He opened his mouth and touched it with his tongue. The material was already damp.

"Mm!" she sighed from above.

He licked for what seemed an age, while Ms Ranjit conducted a conversation in Portuguese on her mobile phone. Then she reached down and pushed his head away.

"Stay there. Until I return."

She left the room. His body ached. He wanted to move, but did not dare disobey.

A few moments later, he heard footsteps returning. A hand lifted the tail of his shirt and lowered his underpants. Then something hard and flat smacked his bare behind.

"Why are you under the table, Blake?"

"You told me…"

"I don't care what I told you," she said, kicking his behind. "Stand up!"

He wriggled out, pulling up his underpants as he did so.

Ms Ranjit was now sitting on the arm of the sofa watching him. She had removed her jacket and opened the top button of her blouse. In her hand she had a wooden cooking spatula and was tapping it against her stockinged leg.

"Do you like cooking, Blake?"

"Yes, Ms Ranjit," said Charles, his eyes mesmerised by the tapping.

"I hate it."

She laughed, dropped the spatula on to the sofa and leant back.

"Take off your clothes."

He hesitated.

"Now! I've a meeting in five minutes!"

He removed his shirt, tie and vest, his body flushing with embarrassment. Then he stood, hands by his side, wishing he had trimmed the hairs on his concave chest.

"*All* your clothes," she snapped.

He lowered the Marks and Spencer boxer shorts he had chosen that morning — for comfort, not display. He folded them and remained with his back to Ms Ranjit.

"Face me, Blake," she barked, giving the sofa a sharp smack with her spatula.

Blake turned and lowered his eyes to the ground. Her high heels clicked across the parquet floor and stopped. She cupped his genitals in one hand and stroked his nipples with the other. He felt his penis grow until it was half erect.

"Not bad for a fifty-year-old," she laughed. "'Half-mast' they call it, I believe."

She squeezed his bottom, returned to the sofa and sat down.

"Come and lie over my lap. Face down."

He did as she asked.

"No need to be scared. I only beat bad boys. And you're a good boy, aren't you?"

"Yes, Ms Ranjit."

He felt her hand stroke his back and bottom and then reach between his legs and squeeze his balls. Not too hard, almost sensually. He began to relax.

"Who's a good boy?" she cooed. "Who's a good little boy?"

Then the hand withdrew. He tensed in anticipation, hoping she might stroke his shoulders. Kneeling under the table had made them sore.

"Ms Ranjit?" he whispered. "Could you possibly give my shoulders a rub?"

Silence.

Then without warning she hit him hard on the buttocks with the palm of her hand.

"How dare you speak without being spoken to?"

He winced and she hit him again.

"Down on your knees."

Charles clambered off her lap, the moment of tenderness gone. The parquet floor felt hard and unyielding to his knees, but he wanted the job.

"You're going to get a beating, Blake."

She pressed her toe against his balls.

"And you deserve it don't you, Blake?"

"Yes, Ms Ranjit."

"For speaking when not spoken to?"

"Yes, Ms Ranjit."

"For talking to a superior?"

"Yes, Ms Ranjit."

"Say: 'I've been a bad boy and deserve to be beaten.'"

He hesitated. The toe pressed harder.

"I've been a bad boy and deserve to be beaten," he mumbled.

"Louder!"

"I've been a bad boy and deserve to be beaten!"

"That's better."

She removed her shoe from his scrotum and sat back.

"Crawl over to the other sofa, lie face down and don't move."

He did as she requested.

The cold leather touched his body and made him shiver. He waited. He heard her swish the spatula through the air. He half turned.

"Eyes down, Blake!"

He tensed his buttocks and, as he did so, she began tapping the left one.

Fast, repetitive strokes, light at first and then harder, in a crescendo of force that brought tears to his eyes. *Bastinado*: he knew the name. A Spanish invention of the late sixteenth century and a form of punishment still used in some parts of the world, though more usually administered to the feet than buttocks. He had read about it, but never imagined experiencing it in person – in Hong Kong, in the twenty-first century.

"Ms Ranjit, please…"

She ignored him and switched her attention to the right buttock. Again, she began softly, increasing intensity gradually but relentlessly until he was forced to cry out.

"Ms Ranjit!"

"Beg for mercy," she said, continuing to beat him at full strength.

"Ms Ranjit, I beg for mercy."

"Again."

"Ms Ranjit, I beg for mercy. Please stop."

After one last hit, she threw down the spatula and sank back on to her sofa. Charles remained in his prone position staring at the floor, too nervous to move.

"Get me my drink, Blake."

"Yes, Ms Ranjit."

He rose unsteadily to his feet. His behind was sore and he wanted to rub it.

"Get on with it, Blake!"

He fetched the drink and handed it to her. Then he stood naked, in the middle of the room, not sure what to do.

"Blake?"

"Yes, Ms Ranjit?"

"Do you think you would like this job?"

"I think so, Ms Ranjit."

"Even if some sixty-year-old wanted to stick Popsicles up your arse and then make you eat them? Even if two thirty-somethings from Korea wanted to pee all over you?" She laughed. "We girls have vivid imaginations."

"I'd do my best, Ms Ranjit."

For $150,000 a month – who wouldn't?

"Good. Now, back on your sofa, Blake. Face up."

He did as she asked.

"I'm going to read you an idea from an American client. She wants to act it out on her next visit. She's a fifty-year-old CEO who likes humiliating middle-aged men while other women humiliate her – weird, but worth indulging. Two Dutch women in their mid-thirties from ABN-Amro in Hong Kong are keen to take part, and a Chinese *tai-tai* is coming in to add local colour. All we need is a middle-aged man. Want the part, Blake?"

"Yes, Ms Ranjit."

"While I read, play with yourself. I want to see how it grabs you."

He took his penis between thumb and forefinger. Ms Ranjit began to read.

"'There's this boss at a desk.' That's you, Blake. 'He calls in his secretary. But instead of the usual girl, two Dutch PAs in rubber thongs and thigh-high boots appear. They undress the boss and force him to put on stockings, girdle and open-crotch panties. They lay him on the desk – face up, legs apart, penis dangling out of the panties like an overgrown clitoris – and lash his wrists and ankles to the desk's legs. Then a Chinese HR official, in a leather cat suit and wielding a whip, drags in an American woman wearing a blouse and flared skirt. HR yanks the woman's skirt up over her head to reveal stockings, garter belt and a pair of lime-green silk panties covering a full sexy behind. The woman is forced to sit astride the boss's face. Her panties are ripped off and the trussed up boss made to lubricate her anus with his tongue. When he hesitates, HR lashes his balls and the first PA grabs his head and jams it into the Yank's crease.' Following, Blake?"

"Yes, Ms Ranjit."

"'He has to lick and lick this tight little hole, with two large buttocks pressed down on his face almost suffocating him. His nose and mouth are filled with flesh, but his tongue must lick – in and out, in and out. If he stops, his balls burn.'"

Charles opened his eyes and saw Ms Ranjit's fingers slip inside her panties.

"Close your eyes and keep masturbating, Blake," she ordered.

"'Then, when the older woman's anus is well and truly lubricated, she is moved forward, head still covered by her pleated skirt, until her cunt is astride the boss's groin. The first PA and the Chinese HR woman – who is also wearing elbow-length leather gloves – pull the large, sexy buttocks apart, while the second PA – who has been keeping the boss's penis hard – points it at the glistening black hole of the older woman's anus, plays it around the rim for a moment and then jams it in.' Wank yourself, Blake. Harder."

Charles hesitated. He felt disgust, but she wanted arousal. His hand tightened around the foreskin and jiggered faster – up and down, up and down, up and down.

"'The man's cock is rock hard, squeezed tight by the older woman's anus. Now, the Yank reaches down, grabs hold of her bugger's balls and cracks them like nuts in a nutcracker, while the first Dutch PA sits on the man's face and makes him lick her cunt through a hole in the rubber…' A luscious, wet Dutch cunt, Blake. Like the sound of it?"

"Yes, Ms Ranjit.

"'...and the second Dutch PA sticks a dildo up his anus...' Your anus, Blake."

"Yes, Ms Ranjit."

"'...and the Chinese HR woman massages the second PA's cunt and tits, while telling her to fuck the man harder, harder, harder – right up his tight little boss's bum...'"

Ms Ranjit now had her legs apart and was moving her fingers furiously up and down.

"Come here, Blake!"

He climbed off the sofa, his penis large and enflamed from self-abuse. He knelt in front of Ms Ranjit. She pulled his head down between her thighs and held it there.

"Lick, Blake. Lick, suck and eat me till your tongue's sore. And if I come, you may get the job. If I don't...Mm!"

Charles worked hard, his own pleasure secondary to that of his future financier. The salary was almost his, an orgasm away – he must not fail now.

After ten minutes, there was a shudder and a groan. Ms Satya Ranjit's gym-fit thighs clenched against his ears and then relaxed.

"Interview over, Blake," she said, pushing his head away. "You can go, now."

Blake glanced up at her face, his mouth glistening, sweat beading on his brow.

"I have the job?"

She laughed and sprawled back across the sofa.

"Job? What job?"

Charles looked confused.

"You're a sucker, Blake. A great big, stupid cunt sucker!"

THE CLEANER

John Evans – mid-thirties, well-built and Welsh as a rabbit – arrived at Chek Lap Kok from Ulan Bator feeling like a stale Dim Sum.

He had drunk too much in-flight whisky and made the mistake of eating an entire 'executive dinner' thirty-five thousand feet above the Gobi desert. Mongolian mutton masquerading as chicken had been his Russian neighbour's verdict, and frequent visits to the toilet had confirmed this discrepancy between description and dish.

Now, he was slumped in the Airport Express rattling through Tsing Yi, anxious to get home and go to bed in the peace and quiet of his Mid Levels flat. A friend from Holland, Henk Bouma, had been staying there, but John had given strict instructions that the apartment be left as found. In other words, clean and tidy with a well-stocked refrigerator and fresh sheets on the bed. Not that Henk would have had to lift a finger. All he had to do was dial a number the day he left and leave the business up to Rose, the middle-aged Filipina who came twice a week to keep John in order.

He closed his eyes and imagined the soft folds of a freshly covered, duck down duvet falling around his jet-lagged limbs and transporting him off to the land of nod.

He dozed through the Kowloon stop and had to be nudged by the stewardess when his train reached Hong Kong Station. He staggered out, clutching his suitcase and laptop, and joined the taxi queue. He took out his mobile and checked the message log. Three business calls from Beijing, two from Ulan Bator and one from his home number.

Probably Henk.

He called up the last message, and heard the familiar voice of his friend.

"*Hoe gaat het?* Just off to the *luchthaven* for KLM flight to Amsterdam. Have left a message for Rose, who says she will do the business. Whatever that means. *Tot ziens.*"

John smiled. Despite Henk's pathological untidiness and inability to wash up or make the bed, he liked the Dutchman and was sorry to have missed him. He thought of taking a few days off and jetting to Holland, away from the humid heat of Hong Kong. But his work schedule was mega-tight, too tight, with no time for tourist trips.

Even tomorrow, Sunday, he had slotted in a meeting with a banker from Tokyo – 10 a.m. at his flat, with croissants and coffee – an important meeting to discuss a joint venture in Shenzhen involving Philips, Sony and a mainland firm. He had met the banker, Taka Watanabe, in Singapore and they had discovered a mutual appreciation of tidiness and cleanliness, so his living room would need to be spotless. Thank goodness for Rose.

He reached the head of the queue, fell into a taxi, cursed the seat belt law and momentarily forgot his home address in Cantonese.

"Umm… *Bowen Do Sa ba m'goi.*"

The driver nodded and set off into the neon glow of a rainy Hong Kong night.

Fifteen minutes later, John was outside the door of his eighteenth-floor apartment inserting Chubb key into Chubb lock. Home at last. Home sweet home.

He swung open the door and reached for a light switch.

Then wished he hadn't.

The place was a tip. Newspapers everywhere, dirty dishes on the coffee table, Coke cans on the TV – even a pair of underpants hung out to dry on an air conditioner.

Henk had been here, but Rose had not.

He looked in despair at the chaos and dialled Rose's number. No reply. He kicked aside a newspaper, revealing a coffee stain on the parquet floor, and groaned. Then he strode through to his study, not daring to look into the bedroom on the way, and hit the replay button of his answer machine.

"Mr Evans?"

A Filipino voice, but not Rose's.

"Mr Evans. Rose is in the Philippines. Mother ill. She tried to ring your mobile, but not working." Shit! Must have been switched off in the plane "She's very sorry."

He slumped into his study chair and put his hands over his face. "Shit!"

His foot touched a newspaper and he instinctively reached down to tidy it up. It was a copy of *Hong Kong Magazine*. A weekly what's-on guide and advertising mecca for lonely hearts, weirdoes and wannabes. Henk had probably been after sex. Dutch men and women were less hung-up about the activity than the English, and regarded ordering up a prostitute – male or female – as a normal thing to do. That would mean very dirty sheets.

John shuddered and was about to throw the magazine into a waste paper basket, when an advert on the back page of the black and white classified section caught his eye: '24 hour CLEAN-UP service! Anytime! Anywhere! Call 2585 6366.'

He hit the dialling pad of his mobile.

"'Clean-Up,' Joanna speaking."

"Hi! John Evans. I'm in a fix. Flat's a tip, important meeting here tomorrow…"

"What is your address, sir?"

The voice was English with a trace of Chinese. He gave his address.

"You have cleaning equipment, sir? Vacuum cleaner, dusters, rubber gloves?"

"Yes. I have a part-time maid, but she's away."

"Fully equipped. Operative only," the voice noted and then paused. "Are you at the location, now?"

"At the address I just gave you? Yes."

"Good. Someone will be with you in fifteen minutes, sir."

"And the charge…?"

The phone went dead.

John shrugged his shoulders.

Cost didn't concern him, as long as the place was shipshape and Bristol fashion before he went to bed. He hated sleeping with mess around, even if – as now – he was dog tired from a week in the outer edges of Inner Mongolia. He took off his suit, jammed his shirt and underwear into a laundry basket and stepped under the shower. Clean and cologned he changed into a fresh pair of white Calvin Klein underpants, a white Bossini T-shirt and loose fitting Diesel jeans. He poured himself a beer and sat down on the sofa.

Should he start tidying? No. Let 'Clean-Up' do the clean up.

When the bell rang, he was half-asleep. He stumbled to the door, opened it and found a small, attractive Filipino woman in her mid-twenties standing on the threshold, smiling at him. Her hair was tied back and her tight-fitting, grey trousers and shirt showed off her figure to full advantage. Over her left shoulder, she carried a canvas bag.

"Clean-Up, sir."

"Yes," mumbled John.

"I'm Juanita and I'm here to clean you up. May I come in, sir?"

"Of course."

He let her in and watched as a professional eye scanned the room. She seemed too slight to undertake such a mammoth task. Henk, a big man, had left a big mess.

"A party, sir?"

John laughed.

"No, an untidy friend. My cleaner's away and I arrived back to find this."

"Must be spotless by tomorrow. Is that right, sir?"

"By tonight, actually. I can't relax when there's a mess."

"Very urgent then?"

"Yes."

Juanita gave a chuckle of satisfaction and indicated the sofa.

"May I sit down, sir? One or two formalities to complete before I begin."

"Please," said John, making himself comfortable on the sofa opposite her.

She took a pad from her bag and opened it.

"Did they explain about the fee?" she asked. John shook his head. "Oh, dear – new girl on the desk. Never mind."

She cast a glance in his direction. This time, as her smile flashed across the space between them, John noticed a hint of mischief in her eyes.

"Mr Evans, 'Clean-Up' allows its operatives to set the terms on which they will accept work. After viewing the task, we set the charge." Juanita paused, glanced down at her pad and then across at him again. "In your case, I will charge $500. But I must ask you to do a few things first," – John raised an eyebrow – "to ensure I work at my best."

"And if I won't?"

"Then I leave the flat as it is, sir."

John felt annoyed. He had asked for a service, now conditions were being set.

"Perhaps I should ring your office and ask for another operative," he retorted.

She returned the pad to her bag and began to get up.

"I am the only one immediately available, but if you want me to leave…"

John waved her back down.

"No. It has to be cleaned. I have an important meeting here in the morning."

Juanita sat and crossed her legs. The material of the grey trousers tautened across her thighs and a calf-length, black leather boot swung back and forth in his direction.

"If you're sure?"

"Yes, yes," said John. "Just tell me what to do."

"Sir, I am a cleaner, but also a person with other needs…"

John closed his eyes. What had he got himself into? Order a cleaner – get a nutter.

"Juanita, tell me what you want and then get on with the cleaning."

"Yes, sir. As you wish."

She reached into her bag and took out a piece of shiny material.

"Please take off your clothes and put this on, sir."

John stared in amazement as she held up a leather backless posing pouch.

"I *beg* your pardon?"

"You want your flat cleaned, sir?" she said, the gleam in her eye hardening.

"Yes, of course I do, but…"

"Then put this on. all right, *sir*?"

John was about to protest when he caught sight of an overturned beer can in the corner and remembered the sheets in his bedroom. If looking at a man in a pouch helped her work, so be it. He'd complain to the agency in the morning. He took the garment and went to the bathroom. He felt ridiculous, but was not ashamed of his muscled body. He took a slug of whisky from a bottle in the kitchen and returned to the living room.

To his dismay, Juanita was still seated on the sofa.

"Aren't you going to clean?" he began.

"All in good time, sir."

He shook his head in disbelief. Here he was, standing half-naked in front of a fully clothed cleaning lady in his own flat at half past ten on a Saturday night, awaiting her next command. Had there been a revolution? Had he missed a newsflash? Was this tight-uniformed, leather-booted, bouncy bottomed woman part of a new working class cadre? He watched her eyes travel down his body, checking it out as he did with girls. At least, he had showered and shaved, and his stomach wasn't bad for a thirty-something.

"Come here, sir," she said.

He did as she asked.

"Now, stand in front of me, sir — with your arms at your side."

He complied with her command. The whisky was taking effect. He was game for a laugh with this goose-stepping Grey Guard — as long as it didn't go on too long.

She stood up and walked slowly round him. Her right hand played across his shoulder and back, and then around his chest, before descending to the flat of his stomach and pausing at the top of his pouch.

He shivered. He hadn't felt a woman's touch for a while and hers felt soft and inviting. She removed her hand and sat down in front of him, her face level with his waist. She ran her hands up the inside of his legs, as if conducting a body search. She cupped her brown fingers over the bulging black pouch and then withdrew them.

"You have a duster, sir?"

"Yes."

"And one of those things for cleaning cobwebs?"

He nodded. He had seen Rose with one a couple of weeks earlier.

"Go and fetch them, please, sir."

He went to the broom cupboard and turned on a light. Even in this small space there was chaos. Henk had managed to upset a shelf of cleaning fluids on to the floor.

Damn him, thought John. And damn this woman! He was game for a laugh, but this was beyond a joke. He rummaged around, grabbed a duster and the cobweb brush with its wavy bristles, and returned to the living room, hoping Juanita would now start work. If the place wasn't cleaned, he could wave goodbye to the Japanese banking deal.

But she was still sitting on the sofa, hugging a pillow she had fetched from the bedroom, her fingers playing with the soft cotton of its cover. She glanced up and smiled.

"Thank you, sir."

She reached out and took the brush, leaving him with the duster.

"Please dust the television, sir."

"But you're the cleaner!" he exploded.

She shrugged her shoulders, threw down the brush, stood up and headed for the door. Again, John thought of the mess and swallowed his pride.

"Sorry. Please stay. If you *are* going to clean, that is."

"I will stay and I will clean, sir. But only if you do as I ask for the next fifteen minutes or so. Is that understood?" John nodded. "*Everything* I ask, sir."

John nodded again. She picked up the cobweb brush and sank back onto the sofa.

"Get dusting, sir."

John crossed to the television and began to wipe the screen. He had his back to Juanita, but could feel her eyes on him. As he bent to dust the cabinet shelf, he felt the cobweb brush play across his back and down between the crease of his exposed buttocks. He tried to ignore her antics, hoping that, if he did so, she would bore of her game and release him from his role as a cleaner's cleaning slave. He pretended to dust, but had no idea what he was doing. He had never had to dust in his life.

She let him continue for a minute and then, putting down the brush, came over and ran a finger across the television screen.

"Call that clean, sir?" she said, thrusting her dust-covered fingertip into his face.

John shook his head, but could not prevent a smile forming. Such a little woman playing the boss! Her hand swung down and smacked him on the left buttock.

"It's not funny, sir. Boys who work badly get smacked. Understood?"

John felt himself blush, though the smile remained. Into spanking, too, were they, this new Praetorian guard of *gauleiter* cleaning ladies? The hand descended again, this time on the right buttock. It stung.

"Understood, sir?"

"Yes, yes…"

Again she hit him.

"'Yes, Juanita, I'm sorry' is what you say," she snapped.

"Yes, Juanita, I'm sorry," he repeated at speed, not wanting to be hit again.

"That's better."

She gave him a last smack and returned to the sofa. He re-dusted the screen. "That's enough, sir. Now, I want you to clean that stain."

She pointed at a mark on the parquet floor to the left of the sofa.

"On your hands and knees, please, sir."

He knelt and rubbed at the ingrained stain.

"Put some effort into it, sir!"

He rubbed harder. She came and stood beside him. He tensed, afraid she would hit him again. But, instead, she played a finger up and down his spine and then reached down between his legs and cupped his balls in her hand. He found it hard to concentrate.

"Keep working, sir."

He felt her sit astride him — back to his head, face towards his bare bottom.

"Has the stain gone yet, sir?"

"No Juanita."

"Maybe you need stain remover?"

"Yes, Juanita. Shall I fetch some?"

"No need, sir. You already have a tube with you."

"What tube?"

"The one between your legs, sir."

John felt himself blush all over.

"Best thing for difficult stains, sir. Pure protein."

He glanced back, but all he could see were her black boots. She smacked him.

"Come on, sir. Get the tube out!"

He pulled down the front of his pouch.

"Nothing will come out if you don't squeeze," she said with another smack.

She reached through his legs and took hold of the tube. Then, with a practiced hand, she squeezed and pulled until the tube had grown to four times its original size.

John felt the patent stain remover start to rise from its reservoir below.

"That's better, sir!" she said "Now, position yourself above the stain!"

He hesitated.

She smacked him and he inched forward, until his now giant-size economy tube was pointing directly at the stain. Her right hand squeezed while her left hand smacked, rather as a child might hit the bottom of a tomato ketchup bottle to get the liquid out.

Smack, squeeze! Smack, squeeze!

The rhythm was irresistible, and he was just about to deliver a dollop of high protein, mutton-enriched stain remover directly on to the stain, when she climbed off his back, knelt in front of him and took the duster from his hand. She laid it on the floor and placed the pillow from the sofa on top of it.

"Please, lie on your back, sir!" she said. "Bottom on the pillow!"

"But the stain remover," John groaned, his tube at full stretch, the miracle cleanser about to appear. "It's coming."

Juanita took no notice and, grabbing the tube, forced John on to his back.

"Better preserve liquid for future use," she said, removing her trousers but not her boots, and jamming a condom over the tube.

"But…" he protested.

But it was too late.

She pulled aside the gusset of her white panties, lowered herself on to the tube – bottom to his face, face towards his feet – and gave a moan of delight. She then leant forward, grasped his ankles and began to manoeuvre him back and forth across the parquet floor. Her groin moved his bottom, his bottom moved the pillow and the pillow moved the duster.

"And that is how we polish the floor," she exclaimed, as, like some human Hoover, John was pushed and shoved from one corner of the room to the other.

"Going to…" he yelled.

"Not yet!" she screamed, clenching her thighs around the tube as they whirled round the floor. "Not yet!"

"Going to…" he yelled, as they careered past the television.

"Not yet!" she cried, reversing his head into the sofa with a thrust of her thighs.

But it was too late.

His head hit the sofa with a crunch, the stain remover flooded into the condom and the tube went flat.

"Now, will you clean?" John gasped, as she climbed off, removed the condom and knotted its end. He was drained, exhausted, and his head hurt.

"One more thing, sir!" she cried, still in a state of great excitement herself.

"The last thing?"

"The last thing, sir. And then I'll clean your flat. I promise."

She stood up, crossed to the sofa, sat down and patted her lap.

"Lay your head here, sir. You must be tired."

John climbed off the pillow, crawled over and laid his head on her lap – his cheek on her clean white underwear, his chin on the soft skin of her dark brown thigh. She stroked his brow; he inhaled the warm scent of her body, his eyes closing as the tiredness of a long day, and even longer night, flooded over him.

He imagined kissing her smiling lips, stroking her thick brown hair – dancing across the Mongolian steppes with her bouncing bottom and shiny black boots…

"Put me to bed if I fall asleep, Juanita!" he sighed.

"Yes, sir," she whispered. "I will."

There was silence in the room.

The gentle breathing movements of her soft stomach soothed his soul; her delicate fingers calmed his brain. Slowly, she parted her legs and eased his head between them.

"There, sir," she sighed, again pulling the gusset of her white panties to one side. "Your last cleaning job. And, please, don't stop till it's spotless."

The warm wetness of her lower lips pushed up against his sleepy mouth, and he heard her sigh with pleasure.

Of course, he thought, as his tongue licked lazily at her own special brand of stain remover – before a flat can be cleaned, the cleaner must come.

Fair enough.

THE BURNING COCKPIT

The situation is out of control, but there is no going back. She is now tying my penis flat against my stomach with a strip of pink silk, and has already shaved my legs, anus and balls and dressed me in a suspender belt and stockings. She says there must be no chance of him guessing my male identity, or he will kill me.

As I say, the situation is out of control.

It all began when she told me about him. At the time, we had been dating for three months and I assumed I was the only lover in her life. We had met at a Celtic dance class in Tsim Sha Tsui, where I hoped to recapture the joys of teenage ceilidhs and imagined Hong Kongers cavorting – as their kilted police bands did – to the wail of bagpipes. But the first class, in a cramped studio in Canton Road, was not what I imagined. Run by a Morningside matron, it was more assault course than highland bacchanal. In fact, had it not been for Mei, I would have switched to Morris dancing in Mongkok. Shorthaired, thirty-something Mei with her perfectly proportioned five-foot frame, sparkling eyes and raunchy laugh was my partner in the Gay Gordons reel and – despite the military-style injunctions belted out by Miss Brodie – I fell under Mei's spell.

She had come to Hong Kong from Singapore to work as a clothes designer and was obsessed with everything Celtic: customs, clothes, language and music. She was also typically Singaporean, with none of the reticence of the Hong Kong Chinese. When the reel was over, she asked me to go for a drink; when the drink was over, she asked me to go to bed; and then, with me on the point of no return, insisted that I continue to attend the Celtic

Dance Society meetings as her partner. And so I have, once a week. And, once a week, we have slept together in her tiny flat above a tailor's shop in Hung Hom. Good, clean, uncomplicated sex. High-spirited lust with moves shouted out in Singaporean English, as if we were at a ceilidh and she the caller. Even her need to play Irish jig music while copulating did not faze me, and I was soon adept at timing orgasms to the final bar.

Was, but not anymore. Two weeks ago, she told me about the other man. She should have kept him a secret. Should have said she was ill and unable to attend the class that week. Should have pretended I was the only one. But she is not a secretive or dishonest woman, and felt I should know. He worked as a pilot and flew in every three months. And, when he came, she liked to be beside his big-muscled, Irish-American body as much of the time as possible. He was the other lover, the one who had been there before she reeled me in with a Scottish reel, before my modest manhood and skinny Scots frame touched her Singaporean skin and tickled her fancy. And, once I knew, I was lost. No matter how loud the jig music, how raunchy her bedroom caller's shouts, I could no longer dance the mystery dance, rise to the occasion and finish the Highland fling.

I was devastated, and so was she. She assumed I was an ex-pat used to bars and bits on the side – a true blue Brit with a joke for every occasion, including this one. But I wasn't, and the more I thought about him, the more I felt unable to compete. He was American and big and brash. He took on mythic proportions, an *urmensch* with powers and potency beyond my comprehension. I began to press Mei for details. How did they do it? For how long? Did she have more than one orgasm? Did he? Was it better with him than with me? Was his cock bigger? Stiffer? Longer? Fatter? Harder? All the destructive doubts that gnaw into the soul and stomach of a man suffering from sexual jealousy; all the questions that a man has to ask, and yet doesn't want to have answered; all the twisted curiosity that kills confidence and can never be satisfied, however much detail is given.

She should not have told me. But she had – *and* told me how good he was, in a gymnastic kind of way. Not to hurt, Mei wasn't like that, but because she assumed I would want to know and share her pleasure. I did not, and could not, and when she saw how much she was upsetting me, she changed tack. He was 'not the same as you,' she said. She could not talk with him, could not dance with him. It was just the sex, and sex was not that important, was it? Well, yes it was, I said, and suggested we part. She would not hear of it. We must work it through. Would she leave him? Well, no. Because of the sex? Because he only came occasionally, whereas I saw her every week – and now didn't come at all, I wanted to add. She was used to him, she said, like a dentist. He meant no more to her than a dentist, but served a useful function, because – to use her woefully mischosen words – 'he filled an empty hole in an uncomplicated, straight-up sort of way.'

"Besides," she added, "he'd be angry if I stopped seeing him. Angry and upset."

"Like me!" I retorted, storming out of whatever bar it was we were drinking our post-Celtic dancing beer that night.

Storming out in a cloud of jealousy, as I had done every week since she told me; Mei running after me, as she had done every week; the two of us making up and sleeping in each other's arms, as we had done every week – babes in the wood with no shots to be called, so no comparisons to be made. Because, I realized, as the weeks slipped by, even if she did leave him, I would still be comparing myself for evermore; still be haunted by his stallion's stamina; still feel him laughing whenever Mei and I took to the floor. The green monster in my head was more powerful than the reality of Mei's assurances and – even if she downplayed his abilities to nil and relegated him to the has-beens of history – she would not be able to wipe his image from my mind and resurrect my body.

"Well, then," she said, one week before he was due to visit, "you'll have to come and watch. See for yourself how he fucks!"

I was stunned, and then laughed.

"I'm sure he'd love that! Lover number two checking out lover number one."

"He *wants* to do it in front of someone. He's an exhibitionist."

"That as well," I sighed, lying back on Mei's tiny sofa and closing my eyes. "A man who can perform in public. Shit! I can't even pee with someone in the room."

"You wouldn't have to pee," Mei said, her face straight as an arrow. "Just watch."

"You're serious?" I said, sitting up.

A spasm of excitement ran down my spine, the first sexual reaction for weeks.

"Why not?" she said, joining me on the sofa. "Only one problem."

"Just the one?" I asked.

"Yes. He only wants women to watch. No men."

And that is why I am now standing on Mei's bed having my defoliated balls separated by a further strip of pink silk and packed – along with my penis – into a wad of cotton wool so that I appear to have a small, but not unsightly, stomach bulge above my virtual vagina. There cannot, Mei reiterates from between my legs, be any hint of a penis, no hint that I am a man. Her American friend has a violent temper, is built like an ox and must be convinced of my authenticity.

"I don't want him ripping it off!" she says, as her hands pack my balls and cock into their cocoon and pull on a pair of elasticated black satin panties to cover the deception. "I'll say you're from the Celtic dance group. A shy, middle-aged Scottish lady who hasn't had sex for years, but who has agreed to watch 'for a wee laugh.'"

"He'll go for that? Won't he want some nubile Asian girl to appreciate his skills? An old hag in a tartan skirt won't be much of a turn-on."

My turn of phrase is light-hearted, but, inside this fancy outfit, I'm scared shitless.

"He likes older women," Mei says, yanking the waist-high panties up more tautly between my legs and straightening the stocking tops. "He says the older dames do much more for him than the young airheads. Particularly their butts!"

"He won't expect me to join in, will he?"

I imagine the American ripping down my knickers and discovering the truth.

"I hope not!" Mei laughs, as she wraps a knee-length, plaid skirt round my waist. "Maybe a friendly pat on the bum, but no more."

"So, why all the detailed stuff underneath?"

"Well…" Mei murmurs, standing back to survey her handiwork, "he may want you to take your skirt off, and then it's got to look spot on."

"He may what?!"

"Arms up," Mei says, climbing onto the bed with a padded bra in her hands. "His full fantasy is this: middle-aged woman, preferably British, dressed in stockings, suspender belt, panties and buttoned-up white blouse, sits and watches him fuck Chinese lady from behind. At the end, she – you that is – applauds. That's all."

"That's all?" I gasp.

"Yes. He told me once, when he was drunk."

I feel myself go faint, as the thought of my nemesis's cock thrusting into little Mei's cunt returns in wide screen imagination with wrap-around sound. My febrile brain is swamped with a sickmaking, motion-picture experience shot in Panavision and Dolby Stereo. I see the stallion, hear the moans, and sense myself – the viewer – a few feet away on the sofa, falling into a black hole from which I shall never return.

"This is crazy!" I repeat, as Mei fastens the bra behind my back and adjusts the shoulder straps. "Crazy! Crazy! Crazy!"

"Of course," Mei says, jumping off the bed to fetch the white blouse, which she has had made for the occasion. "But it'll cure you."

"Cure or kill!" I say, glancing at my bust and realising I can't see my feet.

"Don't worry," Mei soothes, putting my arms into the blouse's sleeves and buttoning it up. "I'll protect you. Now, get off the bed and stand under the light."

I do as she asks and she inspects me from all angles. For Mei this is a theatrical event. The ability of my costume to deceive a red-blooded, Irish-American airline pilot is a challenge to her professional expertise and a chance to prove her skills in a dramatic, rather than purely fashion, context. Of course, she wants to get us back to where we were before I knew about him, but, at the moment, it is the performance and the professional preparation for that performance that are foremost in her mind. In a way, this calms me — makes the situation less insane, less frightening. Like the actor who is reassured by a confident director, I feel safe in Mei's hands. She will rehearse and dress me, undertake the difficult scenes, cue me if I miss my lines — minimal, anyway, as we have agreed I should be a shy lady who rarely speaks — and get me off stage in one piece when the curtain falls. I just have to look the part and stay in role.

To this end, Mei has insisted I spend half an hour each day walking in a pair of high-heeled boots — made to measure by one of her rag trade colleagues — while she instructs me on posture, hip movement and bottom sway. The latter, she has explained and demonstrated, must not be camp and excessive; not a caricature of the wobbling female posterior, but a loose flip-flopping of the *gluteus maximus* to disguise that telltale hallmark of the male: a clenched and 'defensive' butt.

"That's it," she cries now, as I parade around the room in full costume and boots for the first time. "Let the skirt swirl round your legs and feel each step from your hips down, let the flesh of each buttock fall back into place of its own accord. That's it!"

The tight panties cramp my style, but push me into the part. They press against my genitalia and give me an inkling of what it must be like to own a clitoris rather than a dick between the legs. I feel more like a woman and less like Jack Lemmon in *Some like it Hot*.

"Mm!" Mei cries, running over to kiss me. "From the shoulders down you are an attractive lady. If we are not careful, I may lose you forever — to another man!"

I laugh for the first time that evening, and sit down to have my face made up and my wig fitted. Mei's lips are screwed up in concentration, her eyes darting from detail to detail, checking and correcting the slightest flaw. Foundation, rouge, eyeliner, eyelashes, lipstick, blusher; all the elements of a full, female makeup job are called out one by one for my benefit and applied with care and creativity.

Finally, when the brunette wig has been fitted and the full effect of her handiwork surveyed from different vantage points and in different lighting environments, Mei allows me to look in a mirror. I am stunned and, for a good thirty seconds, cannot see myself at all. Instead, I see an attractive woman with a fine-featured face, well-proportioned breasts, long legs and a firm, but not too firm behind. I swirl my skirt and lift it to reveal a flash of thigh above the stocking top. My clitoris strains against the tight black silk.

"This is absurd," I say to Mei. "I'm turning myself on."

"Good," she laughs. "Then you'll turn him on, too."

"But not too much," I add, feeling butterflies flutter beneath my corset.

"No, not too much. Now, have a drink while I change. Then we'll go"

I nod, but still feel sad and excluded. I want to do more than watch. I want to experience what Mei will experience. I want to share the whole evening with her – as a girl. To be in her place, to feel what she feels – to experience that storm of masculine Yankee lust that has chased away my potency. I shake my head and pour myself a whisky. I am getting carried away. Watching will be quite enough, too much in fact. I should never have agreed to go. Never. The situation is insane and totally out of control.

"But unavoidable!" I whisper, raising my glass to the mirror. "Bottoms up!"

Half an hour later, we arrive at the Peninsular Hotel, where Mei's pilot has hired a suite for the night's activities. We ascend in a lift to the thirty-fourth floor and I notice that porters and other guests treat me with more deference – on the surface, at least. In the eyes of some men, I see a look of lust that hints at something rougher, but I enjoy the attention and wonder how long it would be before a man asked me to have sex.

"Here we are!" says Mei, as we reach Suite 3402. "Deep breath and think female."

"I already am," I hiss. "Like a virgin, sacrificed for the very first time."

"And Joan," says Mei, using the name of my Scottish widow persona, "I love you more than him. In fact, I don't love him at all. Remember that, and don't despair."

I swallow and nod. She raises a hand to the doorbell. I hold it back.

"Will you enjoy it?" I ask.

"The sex?"

"Yes."

"If you do," she replies with a smile.

I release her hand and she rings the bell. A few seconds later, the door opens.

He is a tall, broad-shouldered man of thirty-five with curly red hair, freckles on his face and a twinkle in his eye. He is wearing a short-sleeved shirt and beige chinos. His stomach is solid but not excessive, his legs strong and well-muscled. He has on a pair of leather slippers and his socks are white. He towers above Mei and is five inches taller than me. I put him at six foot three and feel myself shrink and shrivel all over.

"Hi, girls!" he beams, bending to kiss Mei. "Come on in!"

"This is Joan," Mei says, after we have entered the room. "Joan. Tom."

"Please to meet you, Joan," Tom says, reaching out a hand and stroking my palm with his index finger. "Or should I say 'Ma'am?' Mei says you're a teacher!"

I blush, but remain silent.

"Joan's lost her voice," Mei says, taking Tom by the hand and leading him to the sofa. "Too much shouting at school. Isn't that right, Joan?"

I nod. Tom sits next to Mei, winks at me and pats the sofa on his free side.

"Take a seat Joan. Mei, get your friend a drink for that throat! Scotch? Or a Jameson perhaps?"

"Tom's more Irish than American," Mei says, as she crosses to the mini-bar. "Only drinks whiskey with an 'e.'"

"'E' for that extra Irish element: Excellence."

He laughs a loud, masculine laugh and again pats the sofa.

I sit down beside him, wondering how long I can keep this up. The panties are digging into me and my nipples feel sore and sweaty under the bra. And what if I want a pee? Mei has kept me off liquids, but nerves can do strange things to the bladder.

"You're Scottish?" Tom says.

"Aye," I reply in a husky voice.

This is the vocal pitch Mei has schooled me in. It is based on the voice of our instructor at the Celtic Dance Society and sounds convincing in small doses.

"All Celts under the kilt?" he booms, putting a hand on my knee and squeezing.

"Aye," I repeat.

Mei returns with the drinks and smacks Tom's hand.

"Joan's here to watch, Tom!"

"Sorry, hon!" Tom grins at me. "Mind if Mei and I warm up, Joan?"

I shake my head, sip my whiskey and try to imagine that I am somewhere else. Tom puts his arm around Mei's shoulder. Mei responds and wraps her arms round the American's biceps. They kiss. My stomach turns and I close my eyes. Why did I agree to watch? Why did Mei think it would help? I am not just a wallflower; I am a witness to the rape of my own self-respect. Mei is mine, not his, and yet now, in her mind and in his – if he even knows about me, the male – I am not here. No John, the other boyfriend; just Joan, Mei's jaundice-eyed friend from the Celtic Dancing Society. And she is a fiction.

"Come on, Mei, Joan's bored!" Tom booms, after a short warm up. "How's about we get down to a real work out."

We move to the bedroom and I am seated on an armchair in the corner of the room. A double bed, with just a sheet to cover the mattress, dominates the space. Behind that, a mirror is positioned to reflect the action. Tom goes to the bathroom. Mei smiles at me, removes her clothes and kneels on the bed.

"Remember," she whispers. "When you have watched, there will be nothing to imagine. All your demons will be exorcised. No ghosts left to haunt."

I shrug my shoulders and lean back in the chair. I want to cross over and kiss her, take her breasts in my hands and suck their dark brown nipples. She looks small and fragile on the bed. But she is not mine tonight. None of her is mine, not her lips, not her hands, not her legs, not her buttocks – not even, once he has started, her mind. She will enjoy it if I do, she says. Well, I had better do my best, otherwise what I watch will not be what she experiences when I am not there, and it is what she experiences when I am not there that I want to share.

"Let the show commence!" I say, a fragile smile on my ruby gloss lips.

Mei gives a thumbs-up and lies down on her stomach, her face at the end of the mattress nearest my chair. A moment later, Tom enters, a towel round his waist.

"Welcome to the main event, ma'am!" he grins, stopping in front of me and removing the towel.

My nightmares are confirmed. Not only is his cock enormous, it is erect and ready for action. It points into the air, high on its own potency and power. It throbs and pulses with energy, straining at the seams before it has even made contact with Mei. Below, two balls hang in a red-haired sack, large and fertile, ready to produce whatever is required. My penis shrinks to the size of the clitoris it is supposed to be. Did Mei ever feel it?

Tom notices my awed expression with satisfaction.

"Look, but don't touch, ma'am. This one here's for little Mei."

I nod, but still cannot remove my gaze from the erect, gentile member and its bulging cohorts beneath. It is as if it is challenging me, challenging me to feel its strength, to take it on – to take it in and tame it. Perhaps that is what all women feel when they are about to be entered. Perhaps that is why size does matter.

I tear my eyes away and reach for the whiskey. I half fill my glass and take a gulp.

"Did Mei mention how I'd like you to be for this, Joan?"

I look up. Tom is still standing there – along with his uncircumcised thing.

"Oh, aye!" I mumble, getting up and fumbling with the zip on my skirt.

"Let me give you a hand," he says, moving behind me.

I feel his cock brush my buttocks as his fingers unzip the skirt. It falls to the floor. He whistles and his cock pushes more forcefully into the silk of my panties. Mei notices.

"Joan's here to watch, remember?"

"Sorry, hon," he says.

I step out of the skirt, sit back on the chair and cross my legs.

"But," he adds, whispering in my ear. "You've got one hell of a butt."

"Thank you," I reply, surprised to feel my clitoris swell at the complement.

And his isn't bad either. As he turns towards the bed, I see his buttocks in close up and want to reach out and touch them. What is going on!?

"Sitting comfortably, Joan?"

I nod.

And with that, he jumps onto the bed, pulls Mei up by the midriff so that she is kneeling on all fours with her face towards me and, without foreplay, enters her from behind – his enormous cock driving up between her legs until it has quite disappeared into the tiny Chinese body. Mei's eyes open wide and then screw up in what I recognize as her look of lust. What takes me ten minutes has taken him ten seconds. He begins to pump in and out. She begins to moan. No kissing or fondling, or preparing the ground. No oiling the seed-drill and checking the bit. The ground is wet, the seed-drill sharp and hard and turning the soil at increasing speed. Mei's breasts swing back and forth, her buttocks arch into her American friend exactly as I imagined they would. Her moans become screams – his grunts become shouts. He grabs her hair and pulls her head back. She opens her eyes and stares at me, lips parted, tongue lolling out. He lunges and bucks and stares at me, too, his eyes boring into the black silk between my legs, his tongue making obscene licking movements. They are both getting high on me: he, on a middle-aged, black-satin butt – she, on a costume good enough to deceive.

I uncross my legs. Tom's eyes widen, Mei climaxes – much faster than she ever has with me, more totally than she ever has with me – and I can take it no longer. I run to the bathroom, close the door, sit on the toilet and burst into tears. I will never forget what I have seen. Never be able to enter Mei again. Never be able to compete. I feel alone and excluded, my body wracked with jealousy and impotent desire. I want to go home, but I want to belong – to be part of the game, to be inside, not outside, of what they are feeling. I want to be him and I want to be her. I don't want to be me.

"Joan?"

A tap on the door, and Mei's voice breaks into my despair.

"Joan. Let me in."

I reach across and unlock the door. Mei, still naked, bursts in, relocks the door and kneels on the floor in front of me.

"What's the matter, John?"

"I want to go home," I sob.

"You've seen enough?"

"I've seen too much."

"But that's all there is," Mei says. "Nightmare revealed as no nightmare at all."

"It's not like with me," I splutter. "He's big and he's strong. He's a man."

"It's not like with you, no. Not tender, not loving, not soft and not warm."

"Not soft!" I hiss. "Not bloody soft – hard as rock. Hard as a bloody rock."

And, again, I burst into tears.

"What else can I do?" cries Mei. "There's nothing else to see. That's all we do. Aerobic fucking four times a year. Would you rather have that than love once a week?"

"If I could do that, would you still want to see him?"

Mei shrugs her shoulders.

"But you can't. And if you could, you wouldn't be who you are – the man I love."

I shake my head and bury my face in my hands. She's right, I've seen it: a display of gymnastics, and that's all there is to see, all there is to it. But I still can't feel it, and it's the feeling she feels when he's filling her body that eats me up inside, that haunts my loins. It's a feeling I can't give her, and a feeling I can't experience. Something she gets from him that I can never give, or have. I'm back where I started. I want to be her. I want to be him. I do not want to be me.

There is a knock on the door.

"Mei, hon," booms big bad Tom. "Can I have a word?"

Mei pats me on the knee and slips out. I hear her and Tom whispering. After a minute, she returns and sits on the edge of the bathtub. She is smiling to herself.

"Why are you laughing?" I ask, miffed that my misery is a cause of mirth.

"He wants to fuck you," she giggles. "Said it might make you feel better."

"Fuck me? What did you say?"

"That you had your period."

"Quick thinking."

"Yes and no," Mei says. "Firstly, you're meant to be menopausal and secondly..."

Again, she bursts into a fit of giggles.

"And secondly?" I say, unable to see the humorous side of the situation.

"Secondly, he said: 'Not a problem, babe. Wanna fuck her butt, not her fanny.'"

The giggles return. I stare at my high-heel boots and try not to faint.

"Anal sex?"

"That's another name for it."

"What did you say?"

"I said I'd ask, but that, if you were like me, you'd say no."

"Like you?"

"I won't let him do it – too painful. That's why he wants you."

"Shit."

"Exactly."

Mei laughs again and then starts to sob. I put my arms around her.

"I'm sorry," she says, "I shouldn't have put you up to this, shouldn't have brought you here. Now I will lose you, and probably him, too."

I stroke her hair and then see a solution.

"Let's share him!" I say. "Just this once. After that, I'll be fine."

Mei looks up at me with reddened eyes.

"Share him? What do you mean?"

I explain about my need to experience what she experiences, my need to be part of what they are doing, not just a spectator.

I say that watching made me feel lonelier, more pathetic, more outside of their lust than when such scenes were imagined. I explain that sharing him – sharing the physical experience of him – may be the only way to exorcise his potency, his effect on my libido; the only way to release my paranoia, give Mei back her gentle but functioning once-a-week lover and satisfy all concerned.

"You want him to fuck you?" Mei gasps, after unravelling what I am trying to say.

"I think so."

"You'd better be sure."

There is a knock on the door.

"Hey, girls?" booms the singsong voice. "Irish boy's getting lo-o-nesome."

"Won't be long," I call and then, under my breath: "Can you fix it?"

"Fix what?"

"Fix my clothes – so that he can get at my anus without noticing my cock."

"You're mad," Mei says. "If he finds out you're a man, you're a dead man."

"He won't. I will only agree to his request on certain conditions."

I explain these to Mei in some detail. By the end she is sceptical of the plan, but aroused and willing to have a go. It is a challenge to her costumier's skills and such challenges she can never resist. She fetches her bag from the bedroom and tells Tom to be patient while the women undertake some 'adjustments' to cater for his request. The bag contains her repair kit and she is soon busy with scissors, pins, needle and thread. First, she cuts a circle from the back of my panties, so that the lower half of my behind is exposed. Then she tucks and sews the remnants of the gusset under the cocoon of cotton wool that hides my balls and penis. She adds extra padding in the lower section and says she will tell Tom to keep his hands off that area as it contains my sanitary pad.

When she is done, I have an exposed anus, but also a credible covered area to the front, where my womanhood is doing its monthly thing in a no-entry zone.

"Sure you're up for this?" Mei asks.

"If you and he do things the way I've described."

Mei shakes her head and stands up. She takes off my blouse, rummages in her bag and pulls out a Lycra top. She slips this on over my bra to ensure nothing comes loose and resets the breasts. She replaces the blouse, refreshes the make-up and gives me a kiss.

"See you on the bed," she says. "And promise me one thing?"

"What's that?"

"If it gets too much, scream!"

"You'll never hear me."

"I will," she says. "Promise?"

I nod.

It takes her five minutes to explain my proposal to Tom. I hear him whistle, and once or twice he laughs. But it is a respectful laugh, along the lines of: 'This old girl sure knows what she wants, and I'll do my damnedest to give it to her.' My nerves return. I am about to enter a new world, to enter my world, to enter Mei's world with him – to share the man who has haunted me for the last three months. I am opening myself up to him, in order to become him and be her at the same time. Probably impossible, but I love Mei enough to do it and love is what brought me here.

"Joan?" It is Tom knocking on the door. "We're ready."

"Aye," I croak and, taking a deep breath, leave my sanctuary.

As requested, a single lamp lights the bedroom. Mei and Tom stand either side of the bed, naked. I pause in the bathroom doorway, hands on hips, taking in the scene. Tom's eyes travel down my body and his cock moves upwards.

"Turn around, Joan," he booms.

I do as he asks and hear him whistle as my semi naked buttocks come in to view.

"You ever done this before?" he asks. I shake my head. "But you're all right about it – as long as we stick to the rules?" I nod. "Mei told me about the breast op. Bad luck, but your butt sure makes up for any loss."

I walk across to the bed, conscious of Tom's eyes on my behind, conscious of his fully erect member pointing at the ceiling. Without removing my boots, I lie down on my back with my head at the foot of the bed and feel my clitoris stir in its cocoon. I hope the padding is sufficient to give the impression of a belly. In the mirror, I see myself stretched out like a grand mum in some perverted porn movie – brunette hair in place, white blouse buttoned to the neck, black panties with vaginal bulge, suspenders over white thighs, black stockings and calf-length boots. I feel at one with the image, not alienated as I did before. I have taken on the part of Mei and am experiencing her power over Tom, her power to set the beast in motion. Mei kneels over my face and breaks the frozen frame. She places her hands either side of my stomach, her head pointing at my feet, her knees tucked into my shoulders. Her vagina is directly above me, three or four inches from my eyes and, even in the half-light, I can see it is wet. I want to kiss it, as I have done many times before, but just then a shadow falls across the smooth skin of her behind and the American's cock and balls loom above my face, too. A hand covered with red fuzzy hair takes hold of the long, thick, impossibly hard member and inserts it into Mei's cunt. She moans and the low-slung balls sway back and forth against her exposed clitoris like the metal balls of a sixties desk-top executive toy.

I take a deep breath and smell her scent and his sweat. It is almost too much, but the sights and smells – and overall sensation of being present in close-up at the moment most upsetting to me in my imaginings of the past three months – stimulate me instantly. My clitoris swells and strains against the cotton wool padding and tight, black panties that contain it. Maybe it wishes to compete with the giant thing now slapping in and out of Mei – wishes to prove it is not second best, even if not as big. Or maybe it is just celebrating its release from paranoia. Being here is not the same as imagining. When my imagination imagines the scene that I am witnessing, my clitoris shrivels. But now that I can smell, see and almost taste the act of penetration, I do not feel excluded – do not feel jealous or inferior – and my clitoris swells in celebration of a union performed for me, because of me, on top of me. Right bang on top of me, so that I see what even they cannot see: her juices oozing out and falling on my lips, not his; his balls bouncing above my eyes, not hers. No, I realise – as the intensity of penetration increases and the sucking sound of cock in cunt excludes all others –

I do not want to compete. Just coalesce and merge with the firm flesh of his penis pushing in and pulling out, balls banging, scrotum swelling; coalesce and merge with the velvet of her vagina sucking in and breathing out, lips enlarging, pearl protruding – the whole of him, the whole of Mei, the whole of me.

I throb from top to toe and fear I will come within my cocoon; that a stain will seep through the satin and he will rip off my panties and then my balls. But, just in time, the final act begins. Mei, starting to climax, and Tom, with seed-drill straining at the seams, disengage and in a hectic dance of lust rush to take up new positions. Mei lowers wet vaginal lips and parted buttocks onto my face, trapping me beneath a feverish cunt. Tom, like a mad dog chasing a bitch on heat, leaps back onto the bed and, grabbing hold of my booted ankles, parts my stocking-covered legs and pushes them up and back into Mei's arms. They have me trapped and pinioned – a fifty-year old Scottish spinster, and member of the Hong Kong Celtic Dancing Society, allowing herself to be fucked up the arse by an overactive airline pilot and his two-timing floozy.

I feel a draft of cold air touch my anus, and then a jolt as the hard tip of his seed-drill hits its rim. I scream, but at that moment – just as the uncircumcised probe forces open my tightly closed hole and thrusts into me – Mei pushes down with her buttocks on to my lips, forcing me to suck her swollen clitoris and swallow her cock-whipped juice. I scream into her, in silence; America drives into me, in silence, too, deeper and deeper and deeper. So deep that I am being split in two. So deep that my own clitoris – pushing up against the limits of its silk cocoon – is growing and growing and growing from the pressure of its bigger cousin underneath. Far away, in the distance, I hear Mei reach her climax, a high-pitched scream of pleasure echoing in my ears; and, a moment later, from even further off, a male roar of lust and a spurt of hot liquid scalding me inside.

Then I am exploding, too: silently, totally, endlessly. I scream – in silent ecstasy, not pain. The more the pleasure grows, the more I scream – without a sound, on and on, no end in sight. This is no normal orgasm. It starts, but does not finish. It grows and grows, spreading around my body like a forest fire on a dry summer's day, burning all in its path – my balls, my back, my brain. And as it burns, my soul flees before it like a deer in search of air. My body is overheating to furnace level, and my spirit cannot take it, it has to leave. It runs like a mad thing round and round my burning bones, up and down my napalmed nerves. And then, suddenly, I feel it shoot out of me – through my mouth and into Mei, through my burnt-out anus and into him. And as it leaves, I know that my orgasm – my endless ejaculation within the nest of cotton wool and satin – is life's last vain attempt at new creation; semen in search of an egg, any egg; life fighting to recreate itself even in the throes of death. I have come, because I am dying; or I am dying, because I have come – either way, the time has come to go.

And now I pull up and away from my body, and, as I soar, I see Mei and her American friend far below locked in a kiss above the burning embers of a lady-man in black and white. Mei's buttocks clamped upon my face, his member buried deep inside my frame. Kissing, oblivious to my departing spirit, lost in their lust and high on my demise. She said she would hear if I screamed 'Stop!' But, when I did, her cunt cut off the call, and now they kiss and kiss while I fly off to die – alone with my imagination for eternity.

Eons later, I awake and find myself in a pitch-dark cinema with rows of floating seats stretching into infinity. On the left of a vast split screen is Mei's bedroom with its moon and stars, on the right, an airliner's cockpit above an endless bank of clouds billowing in an impossibly blue sky. I close my eyes, although I have no eyes to close. When I re-emerge from sightlessness, I see the American on the right-hand side and Mei on the left, both naked – arms and legs, cunt and cock approaching the camera at speed. And then there is one image – the screen no longer split – with me not watching, but in the image, too, a speck of life shooting from him, waiting in her. And as my two halves meet, all memory fades and this, my last record of a former life, drops from the burning cockpit into the endless sea of time, into the warmth and wetness of my new mother's womb.

THE FRAMING

It was stupid of me to do it. But sometimes I have these impulses and then it is a question of living with the consequences. Though it has to be said that, in this case, I could hardly have foreseen the chain of events that were to unfold as a result of my action.

On Wednesday, I had gone to Marks & Spencer's in Pacific Place to buy a tin of organic broccoli soup, a new line cashing in on the sensibilities of a health obsessive like myself. On the way out of the food section, on the ground floor, I had caught sight of a bright red pair of lacy silk knickers given pride of place in the lingerie department. Why M&S situate their ladies underwear next to the food section, I cannot say, unless it is to convey some subliminal message about different types of appetite. Anyway, the red knickers – or panties, as our American cousins insist on miscalling them – could not be avoided as they had been displayed directly beside the food section exit. And someone like myself, who has always felt an illicit thrill when confronted with lingerie, could certainly not ignore them. As a child, I had found it both outrageous and delicious that department stores so brazenly displayed row after row of intimate garments aimed at titillating and arousing both male and female libidos. It was like being present at some vast orgy, where I was the only boy; the object of a hundred, tight-knickered women's desire; a plaything to be smothered in silks and satins and sucked into paradise.

The red pair was of sheer silk with high cut legs and a discreet ribbing of lace along the front. They were stretched over an impossibly perfect, internally illuminated Perspex torso, the shiny material straining under the protuberance of an over-aroused plastic vulva. Behind, on a rack, rows of the same model hung ready to wear, ready for consumption. I should have just walked over, taken a pair and presented them unabashed at the cash desk where two young Chinese women stood giggling. "For my wife," I could have said, if eyebrows were raised, "a birthday present." But I was not married, and, being a high-ranking, expatriate civil servant in the HKSAR government, I could not lie, unless I had been told to do so in defence of departmental policy. Saying I was buying knickers for my spouse was not being economical with the truth, it was a downright lie.

The knickers were for me.

I could not lie and I could not face the salesgirls. I stood, frozen, staring at the tightly stretched drawers, imagining their cool silkiness next to my skin – knowing I had to have a pair. The girls stopped their banter and stared at me. I pretended to be lost.

"Men's wear?" I said vacantly.

"Upstairs, sir," they replied in chorus.

I was clearly not the first man to fall for the red silk knickers. I retreated.

But the next day I returned with a well-prepared plan.

I could not lie, but I could steal. After all, the British had stolen Hong Kong from China, so stealing a pair of panties was, for a sixty-three-year-old Englishman with imperial blood in his veins, child's play, morally speaking.

It was lunchtime and, as I had predicted, the two girls were no longer on duty and the shop busy. Hong Kongers throng and flock en masse during lunch hour and for new arrivals to the city it can be a frightening time of day. The lingerie section was especially full. Middle-aged Chinese housewives – jostling alongside younger Chinese newlyweds and outsize Caucasians – pulled, patted and kneaded the more risqué items, seizing them by the crotch and squeezing them in the gusset, holding them up for approval by a friend, and then discarding them in favour of more conventional fare. I joined the fray, an empty M&S bag in my left hand, ostensibly trying to fight my way through to the food section. No one paid me any attention, and when, by-mistake-on-purpose, I knocked an object of desire to the floor, it was simply a matter of stooping, scooping, removing security hanger and secreting in the bag. Mission accomplished, I stood up, wove my way politely between the orgiastic knicker-buyers, bought a bottle of mineral water in groceries for cover and exited stage left.

Before returning to my office, I descended one floor to grab a *salade nicoise* at Le Cité, a mock Parisian establishment with an indoor terrace pretending to be outdoors – tacky, but reasonable food and rarely crowded. I found a quiet table and settled down to my *South China Morning Post*. I read a leader on overpaid civil servants and then decided to 'peek' at the booty and have a quick feel.

I put the gold and green bag on my lap and was just reaching inside when a shadow fell across the table.

"Excellent taste, sir," a female voice exclaimed.

I shut the bag and glanced up. A petite woman in a blue blouse, blue miniskirt and black latex leggings was staring down at me, smiling. A store detective?

"I beg your pardon, madam?" I said in a suave civil servant voice.

"Excellent taste. Red silk."

How could she know that? I hadn't even opened the bag. She *must* be a detective.

"May I sit down?" she continued.

She appeared to be Chinese, but her accent was not – not at all. And her face was too angular, her hair not black enough. Would Marks and Spencer employ a store detective who was not Chinese? Unlikely, but I decided to play it safe.

"Please. Take a seat."

"Thank you."

She put down her bag, folded the pleats of her micro skirt beneath boyish thighs and sat.

"Michael," I said holding out a hand. "British."

"Kico," she replied with a smile and a bow. "Japanese."

Of course! I should have been able to tell Japanese from Chinese by now. And the bow – that was a giveaway. I momentarily relaxed – then remembered reading somewhere that the Japanese retail giant Sogo had taken over M&S.

I smiled, playing for time.

"What makes you think I have purchased the article you describe?" I asked.

"I don't think 'purchased.' I think 'stolen.'"

Oh, God. Sogo had not only taken over, but also packed the store with home-grown staff and I was in big trouble. I could talk my way round Hong Kongers. Blame it on the heat, meant to pay, blah blah blah. Hong Kongers were used to the English, still mildly in awe of them. But the Japanese? How did you deal with a land-of-the-rising-sun daughter in a pleated miniskirt and latex leggings? Bow and grovel, or brazen it out?

"Look, I know what you're thinking…" I began.

She cut me off.

"I'm not police. I'm artist."

An artist? A store artist? Some Japanese ploy to enhance productivity and raise turnover?

"I'm on grant from Yoko Ono Foundation," she continued.

So it was John Lennon's fault.

"How did you know about the…" I hesitated. "…the item?"

"Knickers?" She pronounced the word with relish, as if she had just learnt it. "I film you. Ever since you walk into store."

"Filmed me? What on earth for?"

"You look suitable. Colonial remnant."

I felt anger rise. Who did this woman think she was? Insulting people. Filming them incognito. I reached for my phone to call the police. Then put it away. She was not the only criminal present. I'd humour her – remember an urgent appointment and leave.

"Colonial remnant?"

"My project. 'Colonial Remnants.'"

"Your project?"

She reached into her voluminous bag and took out a video camera

"I pick items of interest, oddities that reflect colonial past."

I swallowed hard and refrained from comment.

"I wish to photograph you in more detail. In studio."

Memories of Yoko Ono Cox – as she then was – filming five hundred naked bottoms in the nineteen-sixties flitted through my mind. It was time to go.

"Look, Nico…"

"Kico."

"Kico, I'd love to talk, but I've a report to read at the office…"

"What office?"

"Government work. Very boring."

"Ooh!" she said with a long ascending tone. "'Naked Civil Servant.' Very good."

Very bad, I thought. There had been a record cover, too. John and Yoko's naked bums bared for all to see. Probably a 'must contain nudity' clause in all Yoko Ono Foundation grants, and I wasn't going to be part of that.

"Nice meeting you," I said, standing up. "Good luck with the project."

"I wish to film you more. Please, sit down."

"Look, Bico…"

"Kico!"

"Kico. I'm a busy man and I don't have time to be filmed by Japanese artists on grants from the Yoko Ono Foundation. Find another remnant. Goodbye!"

I grabbed my bag and newspaper and tried to squeeze past. She blocked the way.

"I have tape, Mr Michael. I think you do as Kico ask?"

"Tape?"

"Moving pictures. You stealing knickers! Perhaps police like to see? Or wife?"

"I'm not married."

"Oooh!" Again the ascending tone. "Who knickers for then?"

"None of your business. Now give me the tape and let me go."

I held out my hand and looked stern. She was in her thirties with a girlish feel accentuated by the blouse and miniskirt. Playing the powerful parent might do the trick.

It didn't.

"You can have tape," she said. "When you come to studio."

I sank back onto the chair. She had me cornered.

"Very well," I sighed. "When do you want me?"

"Next Sunday, at two," she replied, handing me a card, her tone now sharp and business-like. "And, if you don't come…"

"Yes, yes." I studied the card. "Lantau?"

"Ferry to Mui O – then taxi. See you there."

Her goal secured, Kico stood up, bowed and, with a swirl of her pleated skirt, left. At the entrance to the terrace, she turned and shouted back over her shoulder.

"And bring your knickers, please."

I shrank into my seat as the entire place downed forks and stared in my direction.

The following Sunday, I put on my smartest smart-casual clothes – navy blue linen jacket, pale blue Versace chinos, buffed cotton Armani shirt, black Rockport walking shoes – and took a taxi to the Outlying Islands ferry terminal in Central.

To comply with Ms Kico's request, I had been obliged to pull out of a Swedish Consulate junk trip to Sai Kung and was not in the best of moods. To make matters worse, as my taxi drew up, I saw an express catamaran pulling away. That left the slow boat to Lantau, a lopsided heap of indeterminate age with an open lower deck, intermittent air-conditioning and a permanent stench of stale perspiration. But I had no choice. I was nervous about the tape, and waiting for the next express might delay my arrival beyond two o'clock. A minute's lateness could land me in jail, and I had no wish to go there.

Arriving in Mui O, I strode across to a McDonalds opposite the jetty and showed Kico's name card to a female behind the counter. Kico had assumed colonial remnants like me were incapable of walking and suggested a taxi, but her address was Pier Street and wasting government money – even reclaimable money – on a stone's-throw, metered ride in a blue Lantau cab seemed, if not a matter for the ICAC, self-indulgent.

"Where?" I said, keeping my question simple.

She was trained in McEnglish, which covered the words 'fries,' 'burger' and 'cheese,' but not 'where.' She called over a male colleague with a Canadian accent.

"Out the door, turn right, then second on the right. That's Pier Street."

"*Mgoi sai*," I said.

"You're welcome," he replied.

Number ten was a five-storey block, beyond a row of open-fronted shops. It was clean but dilapidated. Each floor had three windows facing the street, with a small balcony in front of the middle window. I rang Kico's bell. A buzzer released the lock. I pushed open the door and found myself in a dank entrance hall. There was no lift or porter, but a set of stairs. I climbed to the first floor and paused before the security gate of Flat 1A. I took a deep breath and was about to knock when a voice called out from inside.

"Not locked, Mr Michael."

I opened the gate and inner door and found myself in an even smaller entrance hall smelling of garlic and a scent I recognised as Kico's. The inner door slammed behind me and I was plunged into darkness. As my eyes accustomed to the gloom, I saw, a few feet in front of me, a sheet of blue paper hung from ceiling to floor and fastened to the walls with masking tape. The fit was good and all light from the room beyond sealed off.

I was about to try and pull it aside when the voice called out.

"Stay there, Mr Michael, and look up to left."

"Ms Kico, I'm very hot. May I come in and sit down?"

"Please do as I say, Mr Michael."

I put down my bag and glanced up to my left. A TV monitor, suspended from the ceiling, flickered into life to reveal a balding man in his sixties wearing a blue blazer and grey flannels entering Marks & Spencer's. I watched as the camera followed him to the lingerie department, zoomed in on the knickers and recorded their theft in detail.

"Camera in shoulder bag, Mr Michael."

"Very clever. Now, may I…"

"Do nothing without permission, Mr Michael. Otherwise, tape stay here."

I debated ripping down the paper, grabbing the evidence and making a run for it. But at that moment the image changed to reveal Ms Kico, arms akimbo, in front of the blue studio backdrop paper behind which I stood. Any action of mine would be recorded.

"Please, take off jacket and hang on hook. Drinking water on shelf to right."

I took off my blazer, hung it on a hanger provided and opened the bottle of water.

"Footstool next to paper wall. Please sit, if tired," she continued.

I sat down with a creak of ageing joints and again cursed my stupidity. I should have been sipping ice-cold Tsing Tao beer on the deck of a junk in Sai Kung and debating the merits of Swedish social democracy with Consul Lundgren. Instead, I was imprisoned in the hallway of a lunatic Japanese artist on Lantau, drinking distilled water.

I closed my eyes and thought of the Queen. Then, without warning, a pair of scissors sliced through the paper. I heard the ripping noise and opened my eyes in alarm.

Was she a serial killer, too?

"It's all right, Mr Michael. I just cut hole, so I can photograph colonial fragments – never whole thing. You see?"

I nodded, not seeing at all, and watched uneasily as Kico cut a rectangular hole.

"Put right hand in opening, please."

I did as she asked and heard a camera click. I glanced at the monitor.

Kico was kneeling in front of the backdrop with an expensive Nikon automatic. She wore blue jeans and a grey sweatshirt and had a red silk scarf tied round her neck.

The scarf made me nervous. The Japanese had had a Red Army Faction like the Germans. Perhaps she was a camp follower. Preparing to kidnap me and send a photograph of my hand as evidence, or even the hand itself. I shuddered and studied the screen more closely. On a wall, to one side of the blue backdrop, were photographs of Hong Kong – people and places taken from obscure angles and composed in unusual ways. Each photo was set inside a wooden frame decorated with dried leaves, bottle tops and twigs. Hardly the work of a terrorist, I decided, unless she was one of the new eco-freak varieties. I would have her checked out by the Home Affairs Bureau on Monday.

"And the other hand," she said.

Click.

"Now, take off shirt, please, and place right breast in hole."

I hesitated then remembered the video. I removed my shirt and brushed down my grey chest hair. I knelt on the stool and centred my nipple in the opening. I felt her straighten a stray hair and shivered. I had sensitive nipples for an old man and it felt strange having them touched in this way by a young woman. I glanced at the monitor and saw a pale disembodied breast. There seemed no connection between the image and me.

"And now hole in stomach. How you call?"

"Belly button," I said dryly.

I heard her laugh.

"Belly button. Yes. Colonial belly button, please!"

An edge of excitement had crept into her voice, whereas I was feeling more and more uneasy. Where was all this leading? What guarantee did I have that she would ever give me the tape? Maybe I would be subjected to her artistic whims and fancies for a month of Sundays? Not a pleasant prospect for a respectable civil servant. If anyone found out about my visits here, it would be all over the newspapers and I would be out of a job with my pension rights removed before I could say Tung Chee Wa.

Click. Click. Click.

"Now left nipple."

This time her small fingers massaged the nipple with force.

"I want it to stand out, Mr Michael. Like girl's *chikubi*."

She pinched it hard and I groaned.

"That's better."

Click. Click. Tweak. Tweak. I was being aroused against my will and felt thankful for the paper wall between us.

After a while, the clicking stopped. The camera zoomed out and I saw her cross to a chair, sit down and pour a glass of red wine. I lowered myself to the footstool and took a sip of water. My back ached, my knees were sore and I would have welcomed some wine to ease the pain. But none came my way. Instead, there was silence, broken only by the howl of a dog and the cry of a baby next door.

"Are you finished?" I asked.

"Maybe," she said. "Maybe not." She closed her eyes and then opened them again, drained the glass of wine and jumped up. "Of course! The knickers! I forgot."

"You want the underwear?" I said, relieved. "In return for the tape, of course."

"No, no!" she cried. "Put knickers on. Communist red. British blue. Very good."

Her blood was up, her muse soaring, creative block removed.

"Quick, put on. Then *oshiri*, backside, in hole, please."

"Ms Kico, I really don't…"

"Please do! Otherwise, police!"

I shook my head in dismay. The wine had opened up a vein of Ono-ish inspiration I did not like the sound of. But I was trapped. I removed my trousers and underpants and slipped on the knickers. They felt cool and soft, and, despite the compromising circumstances in which it found itself, my body responded to the soft touch of silk.

"Quick!" she yelled.

I positioned my behind across the hole and looked up at the monitor.

I saw Kico smooth a crease, felt the touch of her hand. I saw her pull the knickers up to make my bottom protrude more prominently, a red mound breaking through a sea of blue. I saw her make an indent between my buttocks, felt her fingers probe. I sensed penile dementia setting in and bent forward to ease the pressure on my walking stick.

"Fine! Like that."

Again the click, click, click of the shutter, the whirr, whirr, whirr of the motor drive. I felt a cramp in my right leg and changed position. A sharp smack stung my behind.

"No good! No good! You move!"

On the monitor I saw her strike the red silk again, throw down the camera and return to her chair and wine. I felt my flesh burning as her eyes sized up the red mound.

"Turn round!" she commanded. "Turn round!"

With heavy heart I did as she asked. I felt vulnerable. The silk and her hand had aroused me, but arousal would expose me to further madness, I felt sure. I glanced at the monitor and saw her smile, as blood continued to course into the flesh between my legs.

"British bulldog caught in constraint of communism. Yes."

She reached for the camera, framed up, zoomed in and focused.
"Mmm! Struggle of ideologies, I think!"

Click.

"Remove the red!"

I pretended not to understand.

"Remove the red!" she repeated. "Release capitalist power house!"
She was laughing and clicking at the same time.

"Quick! Do as I say!"

I lowered the knickers and felt my liberated flesh push
foolhardily through the hole in the sheet. The camera went into
overdrive. Clickety Click. Clickety Click. On the screen a crooked,
vein-marked, vainglorious member poked out at the camera; its
ancient, hooded head of mottled, over-massaged skin caught like a
trapped falcon by the lens. I watched it stand erect, quiver uneasily
in the garlic-scented air and start to droop.

"No! No! No! Keep big. I want big, colonial power house."

Her words made me, and it, shrink further.

"Play with it! Make grow! Big colonial fragment! Please!"

I hesitated then put a hand between my legs and stroked the
falcon's feathers.

"Faster – like a machine. Like a machine gun – shooting reds."

My hand moved faster and I felt the hooded bird arise. On
screen I saw her edge towards the blue eerie – whirring, clicking,
smiling, licking – stalking her prey, closing in for the kill.

"That's it!" she cried. "Faster. Faster. Until it shoots. Until it
shoots direct at me! Last remnant of colonial power spent! Last
fragment sprayed on Kico's floor!"

And so I was forced to produce a visible result for this Japanese
artist. And, as I felt the summarily summoned semen surge up
from my scrawny scrotum and shoot out towards her hungry lens,
I closed my eyes, too embarrassed to watch the screen.

"*Takusan! Takusan!*" she cried in Japanese. "So much, old man,
so much!"

When she had snapped the last drop and recorded the retreat of
the powerhouse to its modest origins, she made me tuck it away.
Then she photographed the resulting female form with renewed
glee – a triangle of grey, pubic hair, maleness removed.

"He becomes she," she exclaimed, still clicking, still whirring. "Hard becomes soft. Blue becomes pink. Very good! Very good!"

At last, she and the camera went silent. I opened my eyes. The monitor had been turned off. I took a deep breath. My ordeal was over and I could return to the outside world. I would go to my club, have a drink and then cut that wretched tape into shreds.

"You may put clothes back on now, Mr Michael."

"And the tape?" I said.

"One last photo for records and then tape is yours."

One last photo?

"Of Mr Michael's mouth. Old colonial mouthpiece. Last fragment."

I dressed in silence, without replying. Could I trust her?

"Then tape is yours," she repeated, her voice much closer.

"No copies?"

"No copies."

"Last photo?"

"Last photo."

I knelt down to position my mouth in the hole. But something was covering it. I lowered my gaze. Directly in front of me were the lips of a smooth-shaven, dark-skinned vagina, held open by two fingers to reveal the glistening pink of a pearl-shaped clitoris.

"First I come, Mr Michael – then you go."

And so, I, the spent colonial remnant, licked the coming Japanese artist, whilst, next door, the hungry Chinese baby continued to cry for its mother's breast and the mournful dog howled in time.

SHE AND ME

Up until that day, I had always seen myself as just me. After all, I talk to Myself, I do not talk to Her. I had never considered the possibility of another person sharing my body; never dreamt there might be someone else waiting, like a genie in a lamp, to emerge. It was his carelessness that released her. Without that slip, she might have stayed hidden, and I am sure *he* wishes she had.

The 'he' in question is a forty-year-old, six-foot American called Jason Bush Jr. He has a paunch, fleshy cheeks, thinning hair and no respect for women. He also has the biggest nose I've ever seen. It's not only bulbous, like his figure, but protrudes in a disproportionately elongated manner like the uneaten half of a half-eaten banana. He is married with two children and has been working in Hong Kong, as chief of an investment bank, for five years. I have slaved as his personal assistant for four of those five years.

My name is Brianne Atkins and I am British. I am in my early-thirties and unmarried through choice. I have had three meaningful relationships with well-meaning men, but never felt the urge to settle for the 'monotony of monogamy,' as my younger brother calls it. I enjoy my own company too much and have tended, between relationships, to live in a world of asexual fantasy, where people talk and touch out of tenderness, not lust. Unlike my boss, I am physically attractive and relatively young. I have short blonde hair, shapely limbs and a face – including normal sized nose – that combines friendliness with a hint of severity. Not that I am ever severe, or, more precisely, not that I ever used to be severe. I am by nature a pleaser, which is why Jason Bush Jr chose me as his PA.

I do what is asked of me, and, when necessary, what is not. I solve problems, smooth brows, entertain, don't complain and am always there to pick up the pieces when something goes wrong. Without my efficiency and competence in the area of investment banking, Bush would have lost his job ages ago and be back in the US.

In short, I have been a saint to his sinner, and his temper, abusive language, sexual advances and exploitation of me and my good nature on a daily basis have been accepted without protest and filed under 'par for the course' for *far* too long.

Take the afternoon that led to my discovery of She.

It was Friday, four o'clock. I had been through a long day on phone, fax and internet executing, or rectifying, Bush Jr's investment directives. I had planned a dinner with my girlfriend Amy Chan from HSBC, followed by a not-too-demanding movie and nightcap in Lan Kwai Fong to round things off.

"Not going out this evening, are you, Bree?" came a call from the penthouse office next to my windowless, over air-conditioned cubby-hole.

"Well," I began, wishing he would not – in line with his country's abbreviationist pathology – shorten my name. "I was…"

"Just had a call from Akiro. Wants to drag me off to Macau for a round of golf."

"At night?"

"Warm-up in the Westin bar for a match tomorrow. Wants to leave right away."

Bush Jr's flab loomed in the doorway and lounged against the threshold.

"Sorry, Bree."

I swallowed hard – the abbreviating obsession was bad enough, but to call someone a smelly cheese was intolerable – and fixed my smile in place.

"No problem, Mr Bush, sir…"

"Jason, Bree. Jason. "

He sat on my desk, beer paunch dropping on to oversized, safari-suited thighs – piggy eyes leering at my breasts.

"Got a new boyfriend, Bree?"

"Maybe."

"Lucky bastard."

He made a meant-to-be-sexy-but-actually-disgusting sucking movement with his lips and leant across to muzz my hair. His nose loomed large.

"If you ever get stuck, Bree…"

"Jason," I said, parrying his harassment with a smile. "Firstly, you're married and secondly…"

"I'm a fat bastard" he chuckled, sliding his giant-sized bottom off the desk. "But I can still" – he moved his pelvis back and forth – "…like the rest of them."

"Do you want me to book ferry tickets?" I asked, changing the subject.

"No, make it the 'copter. Akiro's worth impressing."

"Very good."

"And, Bree? Sorry to spoil your plans."

"That's what you pay me for, sir."

A gleam of satisfaction flashed across his face and disappeared up his left nostril. "Clear my desk and hang on 'til the Street's been up a couple of hours. I'm off."

I nodded, willing him out of my space, rang the heliport, booked two tickets and went into his office to face the chaos he always left – on purpose? – for me to put straight.

I found a mound of memos in the out-tray, scattered paperwork on his desktop and unread annual reports stacked next to the computer screen for me to summarise. Then something unusual happened. As I moved his mouse to wipe away a coffee spill, the screen flickered into life. This was a first. Bush never forgot to sign out. He had his own password and I was not allowed to start up for him.

I moved the cursor to 'close,' but curiosity got the better of me.

I opened Word and clicked on 'file' to find the last four documents he had worked on. Abbreviations hinted at content: CEOPREP, STAFFVAC and PERSADTXT. I clicked on the first file – draft memo to the CEO in New York – skipped the second and clicked on the third, intrigued to know what post was being advertised. I scanned the text and let out a low whistle. This was no recruitment ad for Rubin, Rubin & Zwemmer Investment Brokers (HK) Ltd –

this was something more personal:'American executive (38), good-looking and broad-minded, wants to explore submissive side with female (25–35) who's into dominating.' Bush Jr, a submissive side? I laughed. And broad-minded? Broad in the beam, but not in the mind. His limited brain cells focussed on food and sex and little else – though not, according to the ad, on the wham-bam-thank-you-ma'am sex he implied he was so good at. The text suggested titillation for the over-indulged and dysfunctional middle-aged male, what my mother referred to as 'kinky sex,' capers that left me cold.

I shook my head, closed the file and turned off the computer.

But later that night, waiting for the umpteenth call from the umpteenth Wall Street broker, and cursing Bush for ruining my evening, a plan formed in my mind. A plan that She must have had a hand in devising. Certainly it was She who reaped the biggest reward.

It did not take long to find the ad. In Hong Kong there were only two alternatives: the *South China Morning Post*, which I had once used when a new boyfriend failed to materialise organically, and *Hong Kong Magazine*, a freebie left to fester in the corner of fastfood outlets. The ad did not show up in the *SCMP*, so I pinned my hopes on Friday's *HKM*. After all, a magazine that ran an advice column called 'Rough Love' hosted by a gay masochist was more likely to accept Bush's ad than Hong Kong's answer to the *Daily Telegraph*.

On Friday after work, I called in at the Deli France on Gloucester Road. I bought a coffee, grabbed a copy of *HKM* and hid myself away at a corner table. I pulled out the black and white supplement and checked under 'Women wanted.' There it was. I noted the box number and decided to respond by email to find out more. What I would do with the information, I had no idea. I caught a tram home and set up a Hotmail account calling myself Els van Straten. I hoped the 'van' tag might tap into Bush's memory of an Amsterdam trip from which he had returned praising the firmness of Dutch bottoms – female. I had told him it was because they rode bicycles; he insisted it was because Dutch women held the world 'per capita sexual activity record' – information gleaned from one of the *Playboy* magazines in his desk drawer. Whatever, a dominant Dutch dame with high per capita capacity might get him to spill the beans. Plus I had worked in Holland and could speak Dutch – an aid to authenticity if required.

On Saturday, I mailed him a description of myself as a Dutch lady interested in new contacts, ignoring his reference to dominant and submissive in case he thought I was a prostitute. The Dutch tag evoked a warm response on Sunday, but no hint of perversion. He said how much he liked Amsterdam and how he had tried to learn Dutch but couldn't get his throat around the 'g' sound. No mention of an obsession with lowland bums, no suggestion he might want to have his own posterior warmed. So I bit the bullet for him and, on Monday morning, sent a second Els mail – this time from the office – knowing that, at eleven o'clock sharp, he always took a break to check his personal email.

'Dear Jason,' I wrote. 'We have exchanged mails, but you have not mentioned your submissive side. I have a dominant side not expressed with previous partners, and fantasise about having a man in my power. Is that what you are after? Some smacking of the bottom, while tied to a bed – or something more philosophical? Perhaps, you could describe your fantasies, and I can see if they fit with mine. Best wishes. Els .'

At 11.01, I entered Jason's office. As usual, he was checking his inbox. I pointed at the filing cabinet and he nodded without looking up. I pulled open a drawer and watched him from the corner of my eye. His face broke into a grin, then he glanced up and blushed.

"What you looking for, Bree?"

"Dutch contact list," I said, holding up a file. "Must have wiped it by mistake."

"Oh."

"I'll scan it back in."

"Yeah. Get me a coffee first, will you?"

"Sure."

When I returned, Bush was attacking his keyboard. I set down the capuccino, returned to my desk and watched until the frenzy finished. A pause for rereading and then the 'send' button was pressed. I logged on to Els van Straten's account: New Messages (1). 'Dear Els, Thanks for your last mail. Wow! Very Dutch and direct. Caught me on the hop. Sure, trying something like you mention was what I had in mind. But I'm not much of a writer, so maybe it'd be best to meet up and chat first. Know what I mean? Jason.'

Shit! I knew what he meant, but Els was strictly virtual. I fired a mail back. 'Dear Jason, don't be scared to say what turns you on. Words can be fun, no?' He was awaiting my reply. I saw him scan the two lines, sink back in his chair, and stroke his oversized honker. The Bush imagination at work – or what little there was of it. Then his fingers started tapping: 'Dear Els, You know what? I really want to meet you before I say more on this one. And thinking about it, you're the dominant one, right? So maybe you should take the lead in what we do. But writing about it first, well, it might spoil the fun. Jay.'

Double shit! I decided to let him stew. Maybe even turn the heat off altogether. There was no way Els could meet him.

Or was there?

That evening, over a glass of Blue Mountain red, a plan took shape. It was outrageous and risky and not the sort of thing PA Brianne would normally think up. But fictional Els ran with it, and the more I drank the more Els' Dutch courage surged into my British veins, until – with wine and inhibitions gone – I opened the laptop and sent Jason a very concise set of instructions: 'Dear Mr Bush, Please book yourself into the Marco Polo Hong Kong Hotel in Tsim Sha Tsui next Tuesday. I shall arrive at 8 p.m. You must be lying on your bed in a T-shirt and shorts. The only light in the room will come from the bedside lamp furthest from the door. You will not get up when I arrive, so leave the door unlocked. When I enter, you will not move or talk unless I tell you to. Take a laptop and send me your room number when you have checked in. If you wish to accept these terms, mail me today saying, "I will obey your every command." Then no further communication until Tuesday. Mistress Els.'

Next morning, hungover and back in Brianne's skin, I couldn't believe what I had done.

But I had done it. Sipping tea in bed, I powered up the laptop and there it was, at the top of my 'sent' list, a clear invitation to – what? If he said yes, what would I do? I stirred the tea, sank into my pillows and then chuckled. Why worry? There was no way Jason would accept. Fantasising was one thing, accepting directives from an unknown woman to attend an assignation in your underpants quite another.

In fact, so confident was I that the case would be closed, I didn't bother to observe Bush during his mail-checking session that morning. Only later, after a workout at California Fitness with my Japanese friend, Chieko, did I check my own mail. One solitary message for Els, but I was not alarmed – a polite rejection was the most she could expect.

I clicked on the message: 'I will obey your every command. Servant Jason.'

Triple shit! That was my first reaction. My second reaction was more practical. I would call the whole thing off. I couldn't let him spend a night lying on a bed in his underclothes waiting for a non-existent mistress. I wasn't that mean, even if Bush was a bastard. I'd say I had to go to Holland, that Mistress Els had to be elsewhere.

But when I tried to write a get-out note, my brain froze and my body rebelled. Something inside me said go ahead; said I'd regret playing chicken; said that, if I cancelled, I'd never know what it was like to have a bastard of a boss at my mercy. To do what with, though? The surface me didn't have the first clue about being a mistress and no inclination to learn. Would whacking Bush's bum make me horny? I doubted it.

No resolution on waking, but on the way to work I stopped at the Deli France. There was a new edition of *Hong Kong Magazine* and I pulled out the supplement. His ad was still there. Because no one else had responded? Probably. To the best of my knowledge there weren't many women who enjoyed beating the shit out of men – unless you paid them.

That thought led me to the supplement's Personal Services column. Here the masseuses and masseurs, escorts and other sex workers displayed their wares. I'd glanced through it before, but never taken in what was on offer. This time my focused brain picked out two ads. 'British Dominatrix: Leather, Latex and PVC. Toys provided, all fantasies catered for.' Did that mean she wore leather, latex and PVC all at once, I wondered? And what were the toys? 'Domina, tall Mongolian lady. Home or hotel. Full bondage and domination.' I imagined six-foot Bush opening the door of his apartment and finding himself eye-to-tit with the leather boobs of a six-foot-six Mongolian lady who pushes him to the floor, ties his arms behind his back and – what? The ads didn't go into detail, and, even if I had known what to do, low lights and a Dutch accent would not be enough to disguise who I was in the flesh.

Better pull out, I decided again.

But as I replaced the supplement in the main body of the magazine, an ad caught my eye on the back: 'Fetish Fashion – for all your erotic needs.' I had seen it before but never related my needs to its graphic of a woman in a half-face mask and waisted corset, wielding a whip. Now, it seemed like a sign from above. Particularly the mask. If that was part of the gear, maybe being Mistress Els to Servant Bush was not as out of the question as it seemed.

Bush wasn't in the office on Saturday morning. Said he had to play golf at Mission Hills with a client from Beijing. All of Friday he had been in a good mood, with a look of glee in his eye and a swagger to his oversized butt. And why not? He had the easy part. All he had to do was turn up on Tuesday, lie on a bed and submit to the torment of Mistress Els. For him, there was no homework to be done, no costumes to be bought, no 'toys' to be selected. For him, Saturday meant bashing balls around South China's premier course and sipping cocktails in the clubhouse afterwards; for me it meant a crash course in S&M and B&D and anything else that went with being a ball-bashing Mistress.

After work, I headed for Fetish Fashion. I found it beside the Hong Kong Escalator, the world's longest moving staircase, five hundred feet from sea level to mountain slopes. The shop entrance was near Hollywood Road, a block below the California Fitness centre I frequented. I checked the street before diving inside.

I didn't want Chieko, or some other overweight gym-buddy, catching me whip in hand and dildo dangling.

The coast was clear, so I slipped through the curtained entrance like Alice through the looking glass, climbed a flight of stairs and rang a buzzer beside a door. 'First Floor Showroom' the sign read, and then, in smaller print below, 'Fully Equipped Playrooms available for hire in the rear, deposit $1,000HK.' This *was* a looking-glass world.

Once inside, I was greeted by a heavily made-up thirty-something Chinese woman in a black silk blouse and tight leather trousers.

"Can I help?" she said.

"Just browsing," I replied, determined to treat the place with the nonchalance I would treat a branch of M&S – I rummaged through the lingerie there without blushing.

"If you need assistance, press the buzzer. I'm just in the back."

Playing in the playrooms, I thought, imagining a row of naked male bottoms lined up for a whacking.

"Thanks," I said.

After trying to fathom the lace-up boots, double dildos and bulbous butt-plugs, I realised no amount of cool would turn this bizarre bazaar into the M&S lingerie department, and when Ms Switch emerged, I explained that my partner wanted to try out some fantasies.

"Dom or sub?" she inquired.

"I beg your pardon?"

"Your partner. Does he want to be dominant or submissive?"

"Submissive. Very submissive."

"I see. Well, what would you like to wear? Leather, rubber, PVC?"

That same old litany.

"What about something softer, like silk?"

"Not suitable. Let me show you a catalogue, then we make a selection."

And so my schooling in BDSM began, and, an hour later, I emerged with a modest but suitable starter pack of costumes and toys, as well as a headful of 'technical' advice.

"Try out different things. See what turns him on," was Ms Switch's parting remark.

Given the cost of the kit, I was more concerned about my own arousal. For the kind of money I had shelled out, I expected a turn-on, too.

That evening, chunky Chieko came round for a meal. I cooked udon noodles and bolognese sauce and threw seaweed on top. My version of East-West fusion and not the best fare to help a figure-fighting friend. Still, she enjoyed it, and when we had finished and started on the bottle of sesame-scented sake, I posed a question.

"You ever tried S&M?"

"You mean: man ties up woman and sticks dildoes up her *omanko*? No."

"Or woman ties up man and…"

"In Japan, men only get erection if woman tied up, or beaten."

"That's terrible."

"That Japan. That why Chieko live in Hong Kong. You see Japanese porn?"

"No," I said.

"Husband make me watch. Men gang rape nurse, tie up teacher and force *inkei* in her mouth, put wife in cage, whip teenage girl's *oshiri*. No normal men in Japan." I'd touched a raw nerve and prepared to apply balm by changing the subject. But Chieko continued. "If you ask me if I enjoy hitting man, it depends on what man I hit and why."

"You could get off on it?"

"Not in sexual way. But as revenge, *hai*. Beat shit out of ex-husband. Make him shout: '*Itai! Itai!*' Yes, sir. *Yappari. Wakarimasu ka?*"

"*Wakarimashita!*" I said, though I didn't understand.

I didn't think I could hit a man, even in revenge. So why plan on hitting Bush?

Later, after Chieko had gone, I swayed into my bedroom and was about to collapse into bed when I remembered the new clothes in my closet. I made a selection, buttoned, zipped and inserted where appropriate, and then plonked myself in front of a full length mirror. Seen through the eyes of an inebriated me, I looked quite a turn on: thigh-high PVC boots with black silk stockings attached to leather garter belt; rubber thong with fitted vaginal/clitoral stimulater parting buttocks and discreetly penetrating privates; reinforced black-satin bra bonded to breasts and double-zipped at the back.

Ms Switch had gone for mixed fetishes in the way doctors prescribe broad-spectrum antibiotics – to cover all eventualities and maximise chances of success.

And it almost worked.

I took out the flail and flicked it through the air. My boobs wobbled and the clitoral stimulator tried to stimulate. Still not quite right. Still Brianne dressed up for a fancy dress party. I reached behind me for the mask and pulled it on. It covered my forehead, cheeks and nose and had two curved eyeholes to see through. This time, when I raised my head to the mirror, I received a shock. I was no longer there. Instead, an imposing figure, with something of the medieval executioner about her, stared back at me. I moved my legs apart and felt the soft rubber of the stimulater touch my clitoris. I was getting wet and the wetness was lubricating the rubber, allowing it to move freely back and forth. I rolled my hips and bottom, keeping my eyes glued to the figure in the mirror. She stared back at me expressionless, her lower body rotating in langourous circles. I raised the whip and she brought it down hard against her boot.

"Hello, Mistress Els," I said. "Pleased to meet you."

But in the cold light of day, and with a very Japanese hangover, I wished I'd never invented her. The clothes scattered on the floor seemed tawdry, the idea of meeting Bush on Tuesday crazy. Call it off, I told myself. Use the gear on an unsuspecting boyfriend, or take it to the jumble. It had cost a fortune, but some investments pay, some bomb. That's life.

I decided to send a mail from the office. That way I could see Bush's reaction when the butt-plug was pulled.

He arrived late, out of breath and in a foul mood. The meeting at Mission Hills had bombed as badly as my investment. He had bought and drunk several bottles of expensive red wine, downed gallons of jasmine tea, only to be told that the client would keep control of his portfolio after all. He told me all this between dictated sentences of a letter to head office in New York explaining the recent fall in profits.

I was sympathetic, in a secretarial sort of way.

"You got some golf practice in."

Bush stared at me, face reddening, anger filling his bloodshot eyes.

"It's all right for you. Sitting in that office all goddamn day, copying memos and answering the phone. You have no idea what responsibility means."

"That's not quite…"

"No, you fucking don't," he continued, raising his voice and wagging his finger. "None of you fuckers understand. I have to deliver every week, or my head's on the block."

"We do our best," I ventured.

"Best isn't good enough. I'm going to make changes around here, starting with you."

A faint smile crossed my lips.

"No joke, Atkins. I can be a mean motherfucker if I want to."

And for the rest of the day he was – mean as hell. He made me prepare accounts, go out to get sandwiches for lunch – something I hadn't done since I was a secretary – and stay on until 10 p.m. in case head office rang. I was his whipping-girl again, the uncomplaining vessel on which he could vent his overweight anger. He had behaved like this before, but now I remembered Chieko's words: "I could hit a man in revenge." Well, so could I. If Bush was going to be a mean bastard, I was going to be a meaner bitch – on Tuesday night.

Renewed motivation did not remove nerves, however.

What if he discovered who I was? What if he didn't like my gear? What if I couldn't keep up the act? And, more alarmingly, what if he didn't stick to the rules and stay on his bed. What if he tried to rape me? This 'investigating my submissive side' stuff could all be an elaborate cover for an extramarital bonk. Maybe he was a repressed sadist who would grab my whip and flail me, or stick things up my *omanko* as Chieko had so vividly put it. He was a big man, and I'd be hard pushed to protect myself.

With this thought in mind, I slipped into Fetish Fashion at lunchtime and bought two further items, both of which had seemed excessive on my first visit.

"Making progress, I see," said Ms Switch.

"Getting him trained."

"Good. Nothing worse than a slave who talks back."

"Yes," I said, wondering what Mr Switch — or Ms Switch mark two — was like and whether he or she was trained, too.

"And don't forget our playrooms. Some men find the revolving rack a real turn on."

I nodded and left. A static hotel bed would suffice for Bush Jr. Watching his blubbery butt spinning round would be even more revolting than facing it in still-life mode.

And so, the time arrived for my BDSM debut.

Bush had wanted me to work late again, but I called in sick after lunch using 'that time of the month' as an excuse. I needed the afternoon to finalise my script and rehearse in front of the mirror. By six o'clock, I was word perfect and turned on my laptop to wait for Bush's mail. At six thirty, it plopped into my inbox: 'Room 1606. Under Clinton.'

The evening was cool, with a monsoon blowing in from the mainland. I donned my costume at home and covered it with a long winter coat bought in a sale at Lane Crawfords. Apart from the smell of latex, and the occasional unexpected movement of my legs as the stimulator stimulated, there was nothing strange about my appearance. The hotel staff took no more notice of me than usual and I made it to the lifts without incident. Only the mask remained to be fitted. I had not wanted to hail a taxi looking like Batwoman, but nor could I enter Bush's room without it. On the sixteenth floor, I found room 1606 and drew the mask from my pocket. A chambermaid passed. I smiled. She gave me a standard 'Good evening, madam' and carried on. When she had disappeared, I pulled the mask over my head, took a deep breath and opened the door to Mr Clinton's room.

Bush was lying on the bed as requested, just visible in the glow of a bedside lamp.

Good start, my instructions obeyed. I closed the door and stood in the shadows.

"*Ggg*ood evening, Jason," I said, accentuating the Dutch 'g.' "I am Mistress Els."

"Good evening, Mistress."

The familiar American drawl, infused with an amused, almost mocking tone.

"I am Dutch and I am dominant," I snapped. "I give the orders. You obey. Do not speak unless spoken to, and if you do not do as I say, I shall leave. Understood?"

"Sure, Mistress."

"You will say 'Yes, Mistress' or 'No, mistress.' There will be no questions requiring an answer other than those."

"Sure, Mistress. I mean 'Yes, Mistress.'"

"*Gggoed zo.*"

While delivering my opening lines, I had been observing Bush through the slits of my mask. Not a pleasant sight, though he had done his best. He sat propped up by three pillows, clean-shaven, hair combed. A little boy waiting for inspection by nanny. His T-shirt was white and his stomach strained at its seams. His underpants were black with tight-fitting legs that reached to the middle of two obese thighs. Revolting, but I was thankful for small mercies: he wasn't wearing a posing pouch, and he had remembered to remove his socks.

"*Gggoed zo,*" I repeated in Dutch.

I laid down my shoulder bag, turned to face Bush and began to unbutton my coat.

I was in a latex minidress that Ms Switch had squeezed me into and it fitted like a glove, accentuating every curve. It covered my shoulders and upper arms and fastened high at the neck. It moulded my breasts into power-peaks, wasped my waist, and highlighted my hips and California Fitness-firmed buttocks. From there, leather suspender straps led to black silk stockings with embroidered tops, which in turn disappeared into the shiny expanse of thigh-high PVC boots with tight, zipped-up uppers, metal-tipped stiletto heels and pointed toes. Everything in black. Matt black, glossy black, soft black and hard black.

"You like your Mistress?" I said, hands akimbo, legs slightly apart.

"Yes, Mistress!"

Still the amused tone. Still the sense he was in charge. But he wasn't lying about liking me. Between the fat of his thighs, I saw something stir and grow beneath the briefs. A twinge of nausea knotted my stomach and I turned to reach inside my bag. I felt my latex dress rise up, and knew he could see my buttocks. I rotated them and heard him moan. I was turning him on, but was not turned on myself. I might be sexy Mistress Els on the outside, but inside I was still Brianne Atkins of normal sexual tastes and appetite, and with or without stimulator – or irritator, as I now called it – I did not see the current scenario firing me up. Bush was, without exception, the least desirable man I had ever laid eyes on.

I drew out the flail.

"On your stomach," I commanded.

Bush's bulk shifted down the bed and rolled over. His vast bottom strained inside the briefs and induced a second twinge of nausea. Forget the sex, I thought, and think of revenge. This is your boss's bum, he's been giving you a hard time and you have the whip hand. What are you going to do? Run and hide?

I raised my arm and brought the flail down hard on his buttocks.

"You're too fat, aren't you?" I said, as his flesh quivered in pleasure – or was it pain?

"Sure am, Mistress."

I hit him again, as hard as I could, three times.

"'Yes, Mistress!' 'Yes, Mistress!' 'Yes, Mistress!'" I repeated with each blow.

His bottom wobbled, but his sighs were sighs of enjoyment not suffering. According to Ms Switch, the flails were designed to be harmless, unless flicked in a certain manner at bare skin. Through material they had little effect, and, anyway, the flick took practice.

I issued a new command.

"Lower your pants, Jason."

Seconds later, I wished I hadn't.

Two mounds of mottled flesh emerged from his briefs and stared up at me, wobbling like jellyfish on a night out. I reached into my bag and took out a leather riding switch with a thong attached.

The kind jockeys use to urge on their steads. This he would feel. I played the thong up and down the cavernous crevice that distinguished left blob from right blob. I poked it between his legs and wiggled it against his balls. He groaned and put his hand under his stomach.

"Hands on the pillow!" I commanded, hitting him hard across the buttocks.

"Ouch! Hey, steady on…"

At last, a protest.

"You want me to go?"

"No, but… easy does it, eh?"

His body was tense now, on guard, not sure what was coming next. For the first time, I felt a spark of excitment flash through my body. Someone was stirring in there and it wasn't me. I hit him again, less forcefully, parallel with the red weal formed by the first blow. As the hard leather hit his soft flesh for a second time, his hands gripped the edge of the pillow above his head and he grunted. I would have to be careful. He was lying on the bed without restraint, and, if I went too far, he might jump up and attack me. I had experience of the Bush temper; it could flare up like a tropical storm. I must give him some pleasure before the next bout of pain. I reached inside my bag and drew out a pair of skin-tight, black rubber gloves. I rolled them onto my hands and forearms, until only a small area of flesh at the elbow remained exposed between glove and dress. Then, taking a deep breath and closing my eyes, I reached between the lower end of his twin blobs and found his balls.

I cupped them in rubber fingers and squeezed gently.

"*Ggg*oing to be a *ggg*ood boy, are we?" I cooed, my Dutch accent thickening.

"Yes, Mistress."

"Like having your balls fondled?"

"Yes, Mistress."

His body began to arch with excitment. A hand moved down from the pillow and felt around for my body. I evaded it, gave a final fondle to his hairy ball bag – which, even through a glove, felt like the rear end of a plucked chicken – and withdrew my hand.

"More of that later," I whispered. "IF you behave and do as I tell you."

"Yes, Mistress," he said, returning his arm to the pillow.

"Pull up your pants," I said, "and roll over."

He obeyed. The bulge had grown to sausage size. His lust was on the rise and, I suspected, the limit of his submissiveness at hand. I reached in my bag and produced four restrainers. Each had a loop for the victim's wrists and ankles and a metal clip for fastening to the legs of a bed. I hoped this one wasn't legless.

I ran my hand up Bush's inner thigh, around the pork sausage and on up to his chest.

"Remove your shirt, and lie with arms and legs pointing to the bed's four corners."

He did as he was told. I attached the loops to his outstreched limbs, fastened the clips to the bed castors and tightened each cord with the fitted ratchet, noting that the more I restrained him, the more his sausage grew. Maybe he *was* a masochist.

"Too tight?" I asked, when his arms and legs were secured.

"No, Mistress."

"Can you move?"

He could arch his middrift with difficulty, but that was all.

"No, Mistress."

"*Goed zo.*"

I picked up my flail and his eyes followed me as I walked round the bed – or rather they followed my crotch and bum. I leant over him and tweaked his left nipple with my gloved hand. He groaned. I pinched his right nipple, more forcefully. He groaned again.

"That sure is good, Mistress."

I released his nipple, stood back and flicked the flail at his still-covered privates.

"Did I say you could talk, Jason?"

He grinned. I flicked him again, harder. This only served to make the sausage fatter.

"No, Mistress."

For a while I flicked and his member throbbed. But nothing throbbed or sparked in me. It was like trying to jumpstart a cold motor. Flick, throb, nothing. Flick, throb, nothing. I couldn't bring myself to really hurt him and the idea of cold-bloodied, physical revenge seemed distasteful. Perhaps I should stop and go home.

Then he spoke again.

"Hey, Mistress, could you slip my pants down a tad? Kinda cramped in there." Despite restraints, he came across as man at ease with the situation. A leer spread across his face. "Maybe free up an arm? So I can feel that A1 butt of yours. It takes two to tango."

I continued to stare, anger rising. I was, as usual, being used by my boss and my boss, as usual, was calling the shots. I refocussed on my motivation: the chance to teach Bush a lesson for all the shit he'd thrown at me. I reached across to lower his pants. Then, at the last minute, I changed my mind, turned to the table and bent over, until my buttocks were fully exposed to Bush's gaze. He whistled. I reached into my bag for one remaining item. The one I had purchased, along with the switch, on my second visit to Fetish Fashion.

"What an ass, Els. Would I like a handful of that!"

"You would?" I said. "Well, first we'll have to stop that filthy mouth of yours."

I turned and held up a head harnass with a spherical rubber mouth gag. He opened his mouth to protest and, in that second, I jammed the hard, black ball between his teeth. He struggled, pulling at the restrainers and trying to spit the stopper out. But I had already forced the harness over his head and was now fastening the brass buckle under his chin. His eyes flared at me, but the only noise he could make was the gurgle of an overgrown baby.

I surveyed my handiwork and noticed that the sausage had shrunk to a twiglet. I pinched his nipples. He glared. I flailed the twiglet. It shrank further. I flailed. He glared. It shrank. But this time, with each flail, I felt a spark fire within me – the splutter of a motor. He glared. I flailed. It shrank. I flailed. It shrank. He glared. And then, without warning, just as I was beginning to worry that I might be hurting him too much, and that the mouth gag might be too uncomfortable, the motor roared into life and She burst from her hiding place.

I had been staring at his nose, watching the nostrils flare each time I flicked his privates, and it must have mesmerized me. Or maybe it was She who was obsessed with his huge honker. Whatever, my last feelings of compassion – and any hesitation about being a bitch to him – were swept aside, as She surged into my loins and brain at full throttle.

"I almost forgot," she said, with a leer far more cruel than the one on Bush's face a moment ago. "You wanted me to remove your pants, didn't you?"

She reached inside her bag, and, as I stood by – a spectator to my own actions – she drew out a pair of scissors, packed by me to release the restrainers in an emergency, and brandished them in the air. She had no intention of releasing anyone. She climbed onto the bed, positioned herself between his legs, lowered the scissors and ran the blades across his briefs. His body squirmed, his eyes filled with fear, his fat wobbled. But he was trapped. She opened the scissors and inserted the lower blade under his waistband. The baby Bush gurgle turned to a throttled scream. She lowered the upper blade and cut the front of the briefs in half, snipping down and round towards the anus. A morsel of sausage and scrunched up scrotum cowered in Bush's bush, not daring to move. She grasped the circumcised head of the petrified penis, squeezed it hard and then pulled the flesh straight out and up, so that the shaft was stretched thin and taught like a strand of gooey cheese lifted off a pizza.

"Cramped was it?" she said laughing. "We can solve that."

She opened the scissor blades and put them either side of the penis. Bush froze, his eyes widening in terror. She laughed. Then, holding the flaccid flesh taut and stretched to its limit, and keeping the scissor blades positioned either side, she manoevered herself around until she was kneeling over his face, her rubber-thonged buttocks inches from his eyes.

She rotated her behind and smiled.

"Great ass, eh, Jason? Well, take a good look."

Bush had no choice, and, despite the danger it was in, the penis swelled until its blood-filled veins touched the scissor's blades. Then, as cold metal hit hot skin, fear fought off lust and it shrunk again. She arched her behind, the penis grew, the scissors touched. The scissors touched, the penis shrank, the bottom arched. And through the medium of my old self, I felt, with every arch of her behind, the stimulator clutch my clitoris, the rubber plug rub my walls, and waves of wetness wash between my thighs. She had us in her sway: the scissors of Damocles dangling, the penis performing, the wetness welling.

Suddenly, without warning, she downed scissors, grabbed the flail, peeled off the rubber dress and jammed her backside on to Bush's nose, forcing the honker into her anus, until only the latex of a thong lay between his flesh and hers. Then, with nostrils inserted, she began jerking back and forth, flailing the still erect penis as hard as she could.

"Ever wanted a nose job, Jason?" she yelled. "A no-holds-barred nose fuck? Go on, stick it up my bum, you foul-mouthed prick. You disgusting motherfucker."

I felt myself reaching a climax. The combined effect of Bush's hooter up my bum, the stimulator on my clitoris and the sight of a stubby penis being flailed by my alter ego were bringing me to the point of no return. Me wondered how Bush was managing to breathe with a ball in his mouth and my buttocks over his nose. She chased the thought from my mind and continued to ride the honker with the full force of my gym-trained butt.

"Fuck, yes! Fuck, yes! Fuck, yes!" she yelled, as the wildest orgasm I had ever experienced surged through my body. Or was it hers? It certainly didn't feel like mine.

And, as we came, I saw a spurt of white liquid shoot out of Bush's penis and spray on to the flails of the whip that my other self was still employing with gusto. She must have seen the emission as well, because it drove her to even wilder whipping and backside bucking. The penis was flailed this way and that until the last drop had been beaten out of it and she had finally finished the longest, most satisfying orgasm of my life.

And then, as quickly as She had come, she disappeared, leaving me stranded on Bush's nose with a sore but satisfied anus and a very wet thong. My eyes closed and I was about to doze off, when I remembered that men often ejaculate in their death throws.

I climbed off the honker. Had Bush expired? Or just come, despite himself?

I peered down at my boss. His nose was red. His eyes red, too, and staring at me with a mixture of fear, hatred and shame.

His cheeks were tearstained and saliva dribbled from the side of his mouth. My gaze moved to his penis, again shrunken and cowering in its pubic lair. I threw a pillow over it. He winced and moaned. He was alive, but terrified.

"It's all right, Jason," I said. "I've finished now. *Ggg*et some sleep, if I were you."

It crossed my mind She might have forgotten to speak with a Dutch accent and that Bush had already guessed the identity of this bitch with a predeliction for nose-fucking. But no, his eyes showed no sign of recognition and, glancing in a mirror, I confirmed that, with my mask still in place, there was no way he could connect Mistress Els to PA Brianne Atkins.

I picked up the scissors. He cringed.

"Calm down," I cooed. "I'm not going to cut it off!"

But only when the scissors were in my bag, my gear packed away, and the winter coat back on, did his body relax. He had had the fright of his life. Mission accomplished.

I headed for the door.

"Bye, Jason. *Tot ziens.*"

He gurgled, still unable to move or speak – thank God.

I left the room, removed my mask and vanished into the night. I would ring the hotel when I was home. Say there was a man tied up in knots in 1606, in need of TLC.

Next morning, Jason called the office from home.

"Won't be in today, Bree. Bit off-colour."

"Nothing serious, I hope?"

There was a pause.

"No. Bashed my nose on a door. Having it fixed."

"I see. Let me know the surgeon. Always fancied a nose job."

Another pause and a clearing of the throat.

"Hold the fort will you, Bree?"

"Of course, Jason. I always do."

On replacing the phone, a twinge of guilt hit Me.

On the far side of my brain, She laughed loud and long.

Somewhere in between, I looked forward to non-nasal sex with an untied-up man.

MADEMOISELLE CAMILLE

Stefan sat and waited. The screams of children at play drifted up from below and a cat meowed in the distance. He had arrived five minutes earlier and she had gone into her bedroom to change. It was a hot, humid night and he was glad she had turned on the air-conditioning. The familiar chemical breeze touched his face and cooled his brow.

He was sitting on a sofa in a spotlessly clean lounge. He was not sure he should have come, but there was no going back. He had met her a month before at a French evening class. She taught at a secondary school by day and was standing in as teacher of his class for three months. She was forty, with porcelain skin and perfect deportment. He was twenty-six, with blonde hair and a well-muscled body of six foot three. He worked as a broker for a German bank in Central. There had been several girlfriends since his arrival in Hong Kong from Vienna, Westerners mostly, but none of them had affected him in the way Mme Chan did. Her sensuous lips and straight-laced look had fascinated him from the start and, as the weeks went by, he had fallen more and more under her spell.

Tonight he had summoned up the courage to ask her out. On one condition, she had replied. After the drink, he must return to her flat and do whatever she requested. If he agreed, she would go for a drink. If, later, he reneged on the agreement, she would lodge a complaint for attempted rape with her brother, who was a police officer and always believed her. He had laughed. She had said, 'Take it or leave it' and walked away. He had watched her heels click across the floor and then run after her and agreed to the condition. They had drunk in a bar in Lan Kwai Fong and returned by taxi to her flat.

He heard the bedroom door open and, Camille Chan, a tall Chinese woman of slim build, walked across the room and stood at the window. Her parents, she had told him, were from the French concession in Shanghai and she had been brought up to speak Chinese, English and the language of the colonial master. Tonight she combined oriental mystique with French elegance. She wore a cheongsam-style blouse, evening gloves over delicate arms and a loose-fitting skirt from which stockings descended into high-heel shoes. Her hair – cut square, with a fringe – framed a fine-featured face from which bespectacled eyes observed the world with severity and an enigmatic look of desire.

After a moment, she turned, crossed to the sofa and sat down beside him.

"*Comme vous savez, je m'appelle Mademoiselle Camille Chan. Mais ce soir…*" she paused and looked him in the eye. "You will call me *Madame*. Stand up, please."

He obeyed and felt her eyes move up and down his body.

"Stand in front of the television," she said. "Facing me."

He wanted to ask why, but something in her eyes made him do as he was told.

"Here I am, *Madame*."

"*Ne parlez pas!*" she said.

He shrugged his shoulders. She fingered a button on her blouse.

"Take off your clothes. Hurry up!"

He took off his shirt and folded it. He unbuckled his jeans, removed them and placed them beside the shirt. Then he stood in his underpants, arms by his side.

"And those," she said, without a hint of humour in her voice.

He hesitated. In jeans and shirt, even in underpants, he felt on equal terms, but…

"Quickly!" she barked. "Then put your hands by your side."

He did not wish to go to jail, so did as she asked and felt her eyes settle on the newly exposed part of his body.

A smile crossed her lips – a disdainful smile. She stretched out an arm and lifted the penis with thumb and forefinger, as if inspecting the mating potential of a horse.

"Face the wall," she said. "*Tout de suite.*"

He turned to the wall and waited. He heard her stand up, felt her approaching – felt her warm breath on his neck. He half turned his head. Her hand smacked his behind.

"Face the wall," she snapped.

His buttocks tensed, gloved fingers slid up the inside of his leg and came to rest against his scrotum. Again he turned his head. Again the hand smacked.

"Lie down on the floor," she commanded. "*Maintenant!*"

Covering his groin, he lay down on the parquet tiles.

She circled his body, then positioned herself above him – her feet either side of his head, her front towards his feet. He now lay beneath the canopy of her skirt, gazing along stockinged legs and cream-white thighs to black satin briefs stretched tight across a rounded vulva.

"Stroke my legs," she said. "*Mes jambes.*"

He removed a hand from his groin and moved it up her calf.

"Higher!" her voice commanded.

His fingers climbed past the knee and across the white flesh of her thighs.

"Both hands! Both legs! Up and down, up and down – until I say stop."

He stroked. She moaned – but stayed standing. Then she climbed off him.

"Stand up," she commanded.

He did as she asked, feeling the blood rush to his head.

"Take this," she said, dangling a silk cord in front of his face.

He took the cord.

"Tie it round your balls and the base of your cock and pass the loose end back through your legs to me."

Again, he hesitated.

Again, the palm of her gloved hand stung his behind. He winced.

"Do it"

He tied one end as instructed – in a double knot, to avoid castration – and passed the other end back between his legs.

"Kneel on all fours, facing the sofa. *Vite!*"

He did as she asked. She positioned the cord so that it pulled up between his buttocks and across the flat of his back and neck, allowing her to sit on the sofa and tighten or loosen the rein at will.

"Look up!"

He raised his head. She had positioned her legs to reveal the tops of her stockings and the black satin gusset of her briefs. She saw the direction of his gaze and yanked the cord, forcing him to inch closer.

He felt his member grow despite the constriction of the harness. He closed his eyes and thought of Camille's face, the face he had fallen in love with four weeks ago.

"Keep staring," she commanded.

He opened his eyes and gazed at her face in the flesh.

"At my cunt!" she snapped, pulling on the cord until it dug into his anus. "At something you can't have!"

He tried to retreat, but she dragged him forward.

"Keep staring!"

He lowered his eyes to the black satin between her legs.

"Think about licking it. *Comme un chien.*"

She pulled. He resisted. She pulled harder, forcing balls and erection back between his legs.

"Lick with your tongue," she ordered. "But only move forward when I pull."

Yank-by-yank he crawled towards her. In between each tug, she made him pause, stare at the blackness and lick with his tongue. By the time he reached the edge of the sofa his balls were aching and his cock sore, but there was no pat for a good dog.

"Face between my legs," she snapped, tightening the cord to stop him retreating.

He stared at her crotch. He wanted to be held, not buried in her thighs. He raised an arm towards her.

"Do as I say, *chien!*" she rasped, bringing her hand down on his buttocks, now arched upwards to ease the cord's constriction.

He yelped and obeyed. She clamped her stockinged legs against his head.

"Good dog," she said, pulling the cord tighter. "Shame you cannot fuck me."

She yanked on the cord again.

"*N'est ce pas?*"

He nodded and felt her legs squeeze against his ears.

"I don't like being fucked by foreign dogs. *Comprenez-vous?*"

Again the cord was tugged — again he nodded.

"I just like playing with them," she added. "Sit up and beg!"

He squatted on his haunches. She fondled his cock and pinched his nipples.

"Mmm…" she said. "Let's make you a bitch. I prefer girls. Show me your hole."

He hesitated, not sure what she meant.

"Put your head on the floor and your *derrière* in the air!"

He lowered his head and raised his behind for inspection. He felt her gloved hands part his buttocks, explore the rim of his anus and test the entrance for accessibility.

"You'll do as a bitch," she said, giving his buttocks a last squeeze and standing up.

She took something from her blouse and rubbed it in his face.

"*Le slip d'une jeune fille.* Girlie knickers. Put them on."

A pair of pink silk panties dropped to the floor. He stared at them. Again, her hand came down on his behind.

"Just do it, *putain*. And don't remove the cord. *Vite!*"

He rose to his feet and slipped the panties up over his thighs. The silk forced the penis back still further between his legs. She passed a hand over the front of his groin.

"That's better. More like a girl."

She took the cord, now emerging out of the back of the panties, and pulled.

"*Encore sur les genoux. Vite!*"

He returned to a kneeling position. She removed her skirt, but not her blouse. The stockinged legs aroused him and he felt his panties tauten. She positioned her behind in front of his face and, tugging on the leash, forced him to follow her to the bedroom.

Halfway there, she stopped.

"Sniff my behind," she said.

He hesitated too long.

"Sniff my bum, bitch," she repeated, yanking on the cord. "Like dogs do."

He strained his neck up to sniff her behind. He felt absurd, but was excited by the smell of satin mingling with the scent of her arousal. She put a hand on his head and forced his face into her buttocks. Then she pushed him away.

"Dirty girl! Down!"

She was playing with him. Like humans always played with dogs.

In the bedroom, she patted the bed. He clambered on to it. She went to her dressing table and returned with four lengths of velvet ribbon.

"Lie down."

He turned on to his stomach, assuming she wanted to beat him again.

"*Non, pas comme ça!*" she said, pushing him onto his back.

She tied his wrists and ankles to the head and base of the bed. She then removed her blouse, but kept her gloves, stockings, briefs and high-heels in place. She lowered his pink panties and tucked the front under his balls, so that the elastic dug into his scrotum.

"*Fermez vos yeux,*" she said. "Close your eyes. Tight!"

He did as she asked and, despite the discomfort of the panties, felt his penis grow. He opened one eye and saw her watching it. She glanced at his face.

"Eyes closed, bitch!" she snapped.

He closed his eye. Still nothing happened.

Then something soft and protruding touched his lips.

"*Ouvre ta bouche, putain,*" she whispered.

He felt a nipple enter his mouth and harden. He sucked it like a baby.

"And the other one," she whispered.

She made him suck and lick the nipples in turn and then stood up and positioned herself above his body. She had the cord in her hand and pulled on it, forcing his balls and cock to dangle in the air like a puppet. She hummed a tune and made the doll dance in time – up and down, back and forth. She raised her foot and placed a metal-tipped heel on his left nipple. She ground it round and down and laughed – the cruel laugh of a child crushing insects on a summer's day. He yelped and closed his eyes to hold back tears.

"Keep staring at my cunt. It makes me wet to know you want it."

He opened his eyes and stared upwards, along the black-stockinged thighs, across the flash of white flesh to the even blacker tightness beyond.

"You would like to lick it?" she sneered. "Lick my cunt and lick my hole?"

He wanted to reply, but didn't dare. Again he closed his eyes.

"Keep staring, bitch!"

The toe of her shoe clipped his penis. He yelped again and opened his eyes.

"That's better. Keep staring and pretend to lick – like before."

He stared and moved his tongue in and out. She lowered herself until her buttocks were an inch from his nose. He wanted to stretch up and stroke her – take her in his arms and kiss her. He raised his head to reach the warmth of her flesh.

"Down, bitch," she said, flicking his penis back and forth, like a little girl in the street playing with a dog's tail. "Down, down, down!"

Then, without warning, her behind dropped on to his face.

"Sniff me through the silk!"

Her buttocks pressed into his face, her fingers worried his nipples. He sniffed and let the damp silk fill his mouth, unable to breathe in anything but her. She grabbed his penis, enclosed it in her fist and squeezed as hard as she could – a new toy, a new torture.

She squeezed, rubbed, pinched and bent her toy while her buttocks battened down his face and blocked his breath. He strained to release his hands, to return her touch, but the bonds held fast and all he could do was sniff wet silk like a dog without a bone.

After five minutes, she returned to her squatting position, ripped off her briefs and let her nakedness hover above his mouth.

"Boys may not eat me, but you are a girl now and girls like to eat each other, too."

She parted her lips to reveal a red, swollen clitoris.

"*Pour toi, putain!*"

Her wet cunt dropped onto his face and he licked as best he could – a tethered dog lapping water from an upturned drinking bowl.

"Dirty bitch!" she cried, as her juices filled his mouth. "Dirty little bitch! *Putain si sale – si sale*! Next time I fuck you. I fuck you hard right up your tight little ho-o-o-ole!"

A wail of pleasure, a clench of triumph and underneath the upturned bowl, two tears appeared on her lap dog's cheeks.

She sank onto the bed, untied his arms and legs and pulled him on top of her.

"Hold me tight and keep me safe," she whispered, winding her arms around his back, her voice soft and gentle. "*La Camille douce*. No longer mistress mean. *Je t'aime*."

Stefan leant across and wiped his teacher's brow. Within her eyes he saw no lingering lust, no hint of hardness – just a glow of warmth. He bent to kiss her parted lips.

"I love you, too," he said. "*Je t'aime aussi, Camille*."

THE FUNDRAISER

Sunday, at last, and I am able to throw off my shoes and relax at home on the Peak.

Some people regard us rich wives, or *tai-tais*, as spoilt brats. They imagine we only gossip, try on clothes and lunch at the Shangri-la, whereas, in reality, we work hard, particularly in the gala ball season that kicks off after the Mid-Autumn Festival. I love autumn in Hong Kong: no longer hot, but not yet chilly and perfect for *al fresco* cocktails and dancing. Not that I should be planning another do today. No. I am out on the terrace to write up last night's event, and, as a result of the fun had there, am finding it hard to concentrate. My eyes drift across the lawn to a blaze of purple Bauhinias and I make a mental note to ask Felipo to prepare cuttings for our Menton place. I think they'd survive, though they might not like the dryness of the Mistral, that Gallic disaster for the skin. Here we have humidity most of the year and, as a result, keep smooth skin into our sixties. We still do the treatments – to miss a facial with Shukei is a sin – but humid air does the rest.

Anyway, enough on beauty and more about me. My name is Helen Mo-Thomas, born Mo Su-yin – though I'm not going to say how long ago that was, or there'd be no point in the treatments. Like many of his kind, my father fled the Reds for Hong Kong with enough money to start a property conglomerate, Mo-Pacific Holdings. He died in the '80s and left me holding the baby. Not literally, of course, there were boards to tell me what to do, but, as his only child, the company was mine along with the money. I had already married James, a Welsh business wizard of good stock, and I let him take over as CEO, leaving me to spend the excess cash.

I set up trusts to help the poor, as well as war and disaster victims. I supported sports organizations for the handicapped and made donations to educational institutions, hospitals, churches and mosques. I also supported the arts. I built up a collection of paintings, now exhibited around the world on a rotating basis, and, on the opera front, donated to Covent Garden, the Met and Sydney. My greatest love, though, was and is ballet, and, as I am currently Chairman of the Board of Governors of the Hong Kong Institute for Creative Arts, last night's fundraising do was in aid of disadvantaged students wishing to study at the Institute's ballet school.

Because, as well as donating, I fundraise, and, as a fundraiser, I do my best to prize money out of those who are as wealthy as me. Some are happy to give without reward; others, the majority, expect to be entertained. Unlike the taxman (who compels) a fundraiser must seduce, and the most popular form of seduction in Hong Kong is the Gala Ball. It can be anything from a *Soirée Viennoise* to a ballroom event with professional partners, but must always include entertainment on the side in the form of performances, speeches by politicians or comic turns by celebrities. The donors want to be given a good time – as a *quid pro quo* for donating and as an antidote to that bane of the rich: boredom.

Yes, boredom. The rich are forever in search of new diversions, particularly the wives, and it is often wives who donate the most. It is my duty to tickle fancies and ensure wallets fall open. Bored donors feel pressured into giving money and donate no more than the price of a ticket or table, whereas a well-tickled donor participates in the evening's *extra* fundraising activities with a fat wad of notes in his or her hand. The challenge is to find a new form of entertainment and to spread the word that something special is going to happen at 'our ball.' To this end, I form a committee of like-minded ladies each year to plan the event and decide on a cause to support. We set a date, pick a venue, settle on beneficiaries and then focus on organising the night's extra activities.

This year, we decided to break with tradition and go for a women-only ball. Husbands could sponsor their wives (or mistresses) by buying tables or individual tickets, and boyfriends could do the same for belles and has-beens, but no males – unless entertainers – would be admitted. The men folk do not really enjoy gala balls and only come along because their wives drag them there. That is why so many of us have our dance partners: top class professionals capable of providing wives with that sense of elegance and ease lacking in ageing hubbies. There is no hanky panky involved and they are paid a wage like anyone else in our employ, be it gardener, cook, cleaner or manicurist. I have bought and equipped a full-size studio for mine – a twenty-five-year-old ex-miner from Pontypridd called Denis – and he runs a ballroom dancing school there to keep himself occupied and out of trouble when I am abroad. 'Paradise Prancers' he calls it, after the name I gave the studio. Dancing is such a heavenly occupation that I am quite sure whatever afterlife we rich folk end up in – eye of the needle permitting! – it will be filled with foxtrots, waltzes and tangos to keep us on our toes throughout eternity.

But I digress. In order to ensure there would still be prancing and dancing at our all-female event, we decided to ask half the guests to dress as men and half as women – with designations sent out in advance to allow 'males' to practice their dance steps. We debated allowing dance partners to attend, but dropped the idea when I came up with my plan for the central fundraising event.

My inspiration was a movie, *The Full Monty*. I have always suspected that poorer women have more fun than us gilded girls. They know how to party without worrying about image, or whether the next woman has better skin, a more original dress or a firmer butt. We rich girls – especially we rich-as-Croesus, Hong Kong girls – tend to be conservative when it comes to having a good time, and, if I'm being honest, are more concerned about letting everyone know how much the good time has cost than having the good time itself. I was, however, after something more original and daring than a team of male strippers. I wanted to provide an interactive entertainment that people paid to participate in – an event with a party game feel that would appeal to rich ladies with a penchant for lewdness. The husbands have their fun, we know that, and in return allow us to indulge in dance partners, and even lovers. But there is little erotic entertainment for women as a group, even if they have the money to pay for it. Massage by a muscleman, bedding by a beach boy – even humping with a hairdresser – can all be paid and accounted for with our millions, but group entertainment, erotic events of a theatrical nature, are harder to find.

It took a while to convince the committee, but when I assured them that my idea would increase takings tenfold, they agreed – with two provisos: we ask guests to sign a secrecy pledge, and we make the event a masked ball to assure anonymity for participants. I went along with both conditions and explained my proposal in more detail.

Six months ago, I had seen an installation devised by a sculpture student. It was a booth with walls around the top half only. You stepped inside, closed the flap and a hidden camera transmitted an image of your face to a screen on the outside. Passers-by could press buttons – 'Make Me Scared,' 'Make Me Laugh' or 'Make Me Cry'– and watch the reaction on your face as you watched a scary, funny or sad DVD clip visible only to you. It was fun, and my idea was to convert this innocent game into a very adult 'slot' machine that would cost punters $10,000 a play!

When I had finished explaining the ins and outs of my own version of the box, fellow committee members did not know whether to laugh or pack me off to a loony bin. But I had them hooked, and it was agreed to allocate half our budget to the installations.

I came in well under.

Being Chairman of the Governors of the Creative Arts Institute, I can make good use of its facilities. And so – after polite pressure on Deans – the Design, Media and Fine Art Departments combined to produce the required hi-tech sculptures. These were then moved to my studio and positioned on the upper level. This space is bigger than our usual ball venue at the Institute and gives on to a roof terrace with views over the harbour and beyond. The committee agreed to hold the event there to bypass performance licensing laws, and when we did a technical run, I wondered why I hadn't used it before. The room looked marvellous, and apart from my disgruntled dance partner Denis, who had to close his 'Prancing' school for a week, everyone was satisfied. Our only worry was whether it would all work on the night. The game did not allow for a rehearsal. There was a human element involved that could not be rehearsed, and I did not want our secret slipping out.

And so, the night of the ball arrived – last night, as I write – and the committee members, dressed in their finery and disguised by masks, prepared to meet the guests.

There were six of us on the committee and we had formed ourselves into three couples. I had opted for the male role and selected Mona Wong, wife of the Asia Pacific Bank chairman, as my partner. I had also issued dress code guidelines. 'Men' were to stick to the black and white of traditional male evening dress, but could use any style as long as skirts were not worn. 'Women' were to look as feminine as possible in a fifties way and I had suggested cocktail dresses with flared skirts, matching high heels and hair in a bouffant, beehive or backcombed style. Mona looked a peach in a pale yellow satin dress. It had a multi-layered skirt in shades of off-white Lyonnaise, *broderie anglaise* lace trimmings to neck and sleeves, and a matching pair of hand-turned high heels. She had dug out a diamond tiara – last used for Princess Diana's 1992 visit to Hong Kong – and found a matching necklace and bracelet in her husband's rainy day safe. Her bouffant was on the excessive side, but her mask – a Lone Ranger affair in white silk – improved her plain face enormously.

I had spared no expense, and I looked stunning. I had ordered a black leather body suit with matching accessories from McCartney's daughter in New York and had it flown in for local fine-tuning. The foundation garment was two pieces of skin-tight leather joined together by a zip that ran from my collarbone, down between my legs and back up to the nape of my neck. Each half was put on separately, and then zipped together by my maid – a sensuous second skin that moved with my body in a natural and elegant manner. Over the suit, I wore a white leather waistcoat – finished by my local tailor to Stella's design – a white bowtie, black satin tailcoat and thigh-high, PVC boots with eight-inch heels and very pointed toes. My mask was traditional Greek, in reinforced black satin, and covered half the face, with my hair sculpted into a Pharaoh look by Alfonso. I was every inch the domme and towered over Mona, who is a small woman.

She and I had, however, practiced dancing and fitted together well in ballroom terms. She was amazed at how confidently I led and I sent a prayer of thanks to Denis for his efforts. He had spent two weeks teaching me to be the man and, at the end, said I was the best male he had ever danced with. I have to admit that I did get into the part. Being swept around by a man is marvellous, but being at the helm is even more intoxicating!

At eight o'clock, the other guests began to arrive.

Everyone had adhered to the dress code, but none matched Mona and me for elegance and charm. Most of the 'men' had opted for tights and calf length boots and reminded me of Principal Boys in British pantomimes. Top halves varied from black leather, bum-freezer jerkins, to white silk blouses with puffed sleeves and integrated black waistcoats in silk. One or two had gone for traditional male dinner suits and had their hair styled like men. One was so convincing, I wondered whether we should ask 'him' to step aside and drop 'his' pants! Some of the younger ones had opted for stockings and ankle boots and, in one case – the Chief Secretary's daughter, I think – a plum coloured suspender belt designed to look like a cummerbund. The stocking group also wore tails and bow ties and those with oversized bottoms – not a few in our circle – reminded me of Liza Minelli in *Cabaret*. But everyone had made an effort, and the blacks and whites of the 'men' offset the bright silks and satins of the 'women' in a most pleasing manner, with the masks making it hard to know who was who and adding to the *frisson* of excitement buzzing round the room.

The studio had been lit in muted blues and greens and divided into three areas: an eating and drinking zone along the window side, with its magnificent view of the harbour; an open dance floor in the middle, with a stage for the all-female dance band at one end; and a hidden area – behind a bunched drape along the far wall – where the installations were positioned, ready to be wheeled out on their mobile bases at the appropriate moment.

But first we danced – some 'men' more successfully than others – ate, and held the usual fundraising auction, where items like wristwatches, necklaces and *objets d'art* are sold for values far above cost. Despite much goading from me, this raised no more than a meagre two hundred thousand Hong Kong and I whispered to Mona, "Thank God for the special event!" Mona said she was feeling nervous and that perhaps we should call it off. I told her not to be a drip and fetched her a stiff gin and tonic, downing a couple myself at the same time. Mona and I were due to demonstrate the second part of the game and, if I was being honest, I felt a little on edge, too.

After a further spell of dancing, the moment arrived for the *surprise de surprises*.

The band departed, the drape was pulled back and the installations wheeled on to the dance floor by a team of teenage Tibetan girls in leather shorts, white blouses and thigh high boots similar to my own. These darlings had been flown in with special permission of the Chinese Foreign Affairs Bureau and were all certified non-English speakers. The installations consisted of twelve statues of well-known figures from the world of fiction, sport, film and pop-music. They were mounted on mobile plinths and now positioned in profile to the audience on preset marks. Each plinth had enough room for one person to stand behind and one in front of the statue. The figures themselves were life size from the waist down, but with chests and heads disproportionately larger than the lower body. There were likenesses of three superheroes – Batman, Superman and Spiderman; three pop stars – Mick Jagger, Andy Lau and Ricky Martin; three film stars – Brad Pitt, Jackie Chan and Tom Cruise; and three sports stars – David Beckham, Andre Agassi and the Chinese diver whose name I can never remember. They were all standing with their legs slightly apart and arms raised in appropriate gestures – Jackie in a karate pose, Mick with a microphone, Andre with a tennis racket and so on. All had perfectly shaped legs and buttocks and an impressive bulge in the front of their pants.

Behind and above the figures, along the upper half of the rear wall, there were thirty-six television screens arranged in vertical blocks of three, with each block positioned opposite one of the figures on the floor. Above each block, the name of the sculpted figure was printed, so that viewers at the dining tables across the room could identify which set of screens was which. Finally, twin-door cabinets in matte black were set on the floor in front of the plinths and a key to each cabinet placed on top.

With everything in place, the Tibetan girls bowed to the guests and departed. I stood up and walked to a microphone. A spotlight picked me out and I cleared my throat.

A hush fell over the studio.

"Inside each of these celebrities is a real live man!" I began.

I waited for the "oohs" and "aahs" to die down and pressed a switch spotlighting each of the figures on their face, crotch and backside. The guests laughed.

"The men inside – in their early twenties and participating willingly – can neither see nor hear us. But," and here I pressed another button, "we can see their faces."

One by one twelve men's faces appeared on the uppermost of the three TV screens, a little bewildered and nervous looking, but all young and handsome, having been handpicked by me from an agency in Manila. All were Filipinos and all had been brought over to Hong Kong a week earlier and provided with employment contracts as gardeners or drivers. They were each being paid $3,000 for tonight's event on the understanding that they did not divulge – or complain about – anything that might happen in the course of the evening. If they did, the event and their participation would be denied and their coveted contracts of employment terminated. They would then have to return to the Philippines and poverty. Earlier, they had been brought blindfolded to the studio in a coach and, ten minutes ago, positioned inside the statues by the Tibetan girls with whom they had no way of communicating. These girls would return to release the men when the game was over, replace blindfolds, hand over cash and dispatch them back to their places of employment. In the outsize head of each statue was a camera hidden behind a screen, and these cameras were now transmitting the twelve faces for our entertainment. The rest of the statue's body had been lined with a non-allergenic, padded material for the men's comfort while 'fixed' in position. Because fixed they were, with no movement possible – except in one important area.

"The game is divided into two parts," I continued. "Participation in the first part can be done on an individual basis and will cost $20,000 a play, minimum. Participation in the second part can only be done as a couple – in other words, one 'man' and one woman – and will cost fifty thousand per pair, minimum. Participants will be selected on a highest bid basis. Those not participating may bet on those who are – minimum stake $10,000 – and then donate their winnings back to us!"

Scattered laughter, but the twelve men on the screen could not hear and continued to stare at their screens, wondering what was to happen next.

"Game one involves a remote control and monitoring of the action on the middle of the three screens situated above and behind each statue. There are twelve remotes available, so please write down your sealed bids for first 'go' now."

Bids were scribbled on paper napkins, collected and the winners declared. The highest bid was $50,000 and the total raised by this first round of the first game was four hundred thousand Hong Kong – very satisfactory.

The remotes were distributed and I explained the rules.

"On the second screen down, you will see the big bulges of our celebrity statues."

I pressed a button and close-ups of the twelve bulges appeared on the monitors. More "oohs" and "aahs" and a few giggles – I had their attention.

"But what's the use of a bulge if you can't see the goods?"

This produced a hen-like round of laughter – not *Full Monty* raucous, but acceptable. I pressed another button. Sliding doors slid back on twelve bulges to reveal twelve sets of private parts in varying shapes and sizes. The guests roared with laughter, covered their mouths or their eyes, or both, and glanced upwards to the top screen. The faces registered the exposure of nether regions to colder air, but gave no sign of awareness that these were now on show to a female audience. Some grimaced, some smiled, some looked downwards, but could neither see nor do anything.

"Now," I said, "on your remote there are ten buttons and, when you press any one of these, a film will start playing on a screen in front of the men's eyes. The ten buttons relate to different types of pornography, geared to appeal to the various sexual appetites of men and women – though I'm sure none of us view this kind of stuff, do we, girls?"

A loud roar of "No!" followed by laughter and a growing buzz of excitement.

"And to help you monitor what you are feeding your celebrity 'cock' – as I will now call them – the nature of the film selected will be transmitted on to the lowest of the three screens opposite, but NOT the film itself as that might break your concentration."

More laughter and a few cries of "Shame!" from the *gweipos* present. I had already noted that the half dozen white women – all dressed as men – were letting their hair down quicker than the locals. Hong Kong is a moral place when it comes to sex and I sometimes wish we had had the Portuguese, not the British, as our colonial masters. Nineteenth-century British prudery combined with Chinese reticence has engendered a repressed approach to lust, albeit a more subtle and refined eroticism on the surface. Western men praise our ability to combine elegance with sexiness, and that is something Western women, with their cumbersome bodies, find harder to do. However, once we are asked to go beyond image and actually do something, we tend to be lame ducks.

But I digress again.

"Ladies, 'Gentlemen,'" I continued. "A word on scoring."

I pressed another button and two metal prongs with a thin wire strung between them appeared directly above the open groin of each statue. The guests whispered amongst themselves, not sure what to make of this new device.

"As we all know, when a man is aroused he – unlike us more sophisticated ladies – cannot hide the fact. So, if you hit the right button for your celebrity cock, that cock will rise to the occasion and touch the wire above it. Every time it does, a counter will register the seconds it remains in contact and fully erect. The winner is the first contestant to reach three minutes of contact time. Of course, you will also be able to see the results of your handiwork on the middle screens, and in the flesh, but the wires – all set at the same height – will ensure there is no dispute over whose cock is performing best and what constitutes 'fully erect.' Because, I suspect, some of us married ladies may well have forgotten what a full erection is meant to look like!"

Again roars of laughter, followed by clapping and a shuffling of chairs to get a better view of the screens and the nearest statue.

"I now ask the twelve contestants to stand in front of their celebrity cocks with remotes at the ready. And remember: NO touching."

The twelve highest bidders – eight 'men' and four women – climbed on to the plinth of the statue indicated on the back of their remotes and took up positions. One rogue cock popped up, causing the contestant to throw up her arms in mock horror and back away. A glance at the screens told us its owner had coughed.

More giggles and an expectant hush.

"The horses are in the starting gate – the cocks ready to crow. Those wishing to place bets please do so now by filling in a slip and handing it to a committee member. And remember: minimum bet, ten thousand!"

I pressed a button and a fanfare blasted out of speakers set around the walls. I noted with satisfaction that the men's faces on the screens remained impassive. They could hear and see nothing. I felt a tingle of excitement at the thought of exposing these men to our ridicule, of manipulating their young bodies for our delight and entertainment.

"Let the game commence!"

And it did. Remotes were pressed, the men's faces on screen came to life – some laughing, some wide-eyed, others blushing – and down below their thick, thin, big, small, bald, hooded, straight and crooked cocks began to react.

Some players zapped from one category to the next in an attempt to hit the jackpot and the men's expressions changed from lust, to disgust, to bewilderment and back again as ten categories flashed past their eyes – 'Straight sex,' 'Anal sex,' 'Oral sex,' 'Lesbian sex,' 'Group Sex,' 'Sadistic Sex,' 'Masochistic Sex,' 'Gay Sex,' 'Golden Shower Sex' and 'Animal Sex.' The twelve cocks wavered up and down like flags in the wind, occasionally hitting the wire and clocking up seconds, but more often than not failing to make the grade and hanging at half-mast or limp against the flagpole.

The crowd laughed and cheered and placed more bets. Superman was an early leader and seemed to do best on Straight Sex, while Batman preferred Gay interspersed with Masochistic. The man in Mick Jagger responded well to Oral, while the lad in Jackie Chan jumped at Lesbian and the inmates of Andre Agassi and Andy Lau, both slow starters, finally came to life with Golden Shower Sex. Animal Sex caused drooping and a closing of the eyes in most cases, through the boys inside Brad Pitt and David Beckham seemed to enjoy it. In fact, after extended exposure to this category, Beckham clocked up the longest erection at wire height of any cock – thirty seconds. But then something too revolting came up and the lad inside closed his eyes and felt his penis flop. The contestants controlling Ricky Martin, Tom Cruise and Chinese Diver tried a different tactic, feeding all three a non-stop diet of group sex. This seemed to work for the occupants of Ricky Martin and Chinese Diver, but the man inside Tom Cruise was having difficulty getting above half-mast. In the end, his controller hit the Sadistic button and Tom's cock shot to attention and stayed there for a full three minutes overtaking all others and winning the first round.

Two more rounds followed, with remotes cross connected so that players had to work out which celebrity cock they were controlling. Sometimes it was the one they were standing in front of, but more often than not it was one of the others. In this way, categories connected to a cock in the first round could not be reapplied in subsequent ones.

After three rounds, we had raised a total of one million from fees and a further four hundred thousand from bets. One of the keenest players was the wife of the British Consul, Lady Hesketh, who was dressed Principal Boy-fashion in tights, boots and tails. She had on a full face mask, but I recognised her when tailcoats were removed to play the game. She has the biggest bottom in town and its wobble, when using a remote, is unique.

After a pause for drinks and chitchat, it was time to announce the second part of the game, the grand finale of the evening. I returned to the microphone and all eyes turned on me, alight with alcohol and expectation.

"The second part is more hands on," I began.

Roars of approval and much stamping of high heels.

"Though no direct touching!"

Cries of "Shame!" and an odd "Boo!"

"So, to add to your titillation, I will now reveal a little more of our mystery men's identities. Please watch the lowest of the three screens carefully."

I pressed a button. This time doors slid open at the back of each statue revealing an on-screen close up of twelve sets of firm, brown Filipino buttocks. Again the faces of the men showed bewilderment and, this time, more unease. 'Keep your rear covered' is an old military adage and for a man to expose his behind is a risky business – especially with a hundred hyped-up ladies in the room!

The revelation of more flesh was an excuse for the audience to let its hair down even further. *Gweipo* and Chinese alike screamed and catcalled, and one or two tried to rush the plinths and 'have a squeeze.'

"Please, ladies!" I called, bringing the gathering to order. "Look but don't touch. The next game requires couples, with a 'man' behind and a 'woman' in front of the allocated celebrity. That is all I will reveal at this stage. So, submit your sealed bids. And remember: minimum bid fifty thousand per person, or one hundred thousand per couple."

Again, much scribbling of figures before all bids had been collected. As prearranged, Mona and I were announced as couple number one with a bid of two hundred thousand. This was greeted with approval, as were subsequent winning bids – all above one hundred thousand – and the combined total came to one and a half million.

When this figure had been announced, to tumultuous applause, I removed the microphone from its stand, took Mona's hand and walked to the figure of Superman.

"Once the rules are clear," I announced, "other participating couples should take up positions. The next highest bidder goes to the statue next to mine, the lowest to Tom Cruise at the far end, all others to the figures in between – in order of bid size. Clear?"

I took the key from on top of the cabinet and opened the doors. I pulled out a feather duster and leather flail and handed them to Mona.

I explained that she would stand on the plinth in front of the statue and use either, or both, of her implements to stimulate her celebrity cock. But, I added, she could not use her hands – or mouth. Laughter, but also nervous tittering: even without skin-on-skin touching, the event was moving to a different level. They knew that and I knew that, and I relied on my charisma and the group dynamic to silence objectors and encourage the crowd to follow its leader.

I reached inside the cabinet and pulled out a white, six-inch dildo mounted on a pair of reinforced black rubber panties. A gasp went up from the crowd.

"The little difference!" I cooed into my microphone.

I bent, stepped into the leg-holes and pulled the penis up between my legs. The phallus dazzled against the black of my leather cat suit, and I knew I looked good.

Some women giggled, but most stared in silence not sure what to make of it all.

"I, as the 'male,' will stand behind my celebrity and may use this in any way I consider appropriate. To ensure that I do not cause unnecessary pain, I will also use this."

I reached in to the cabinet and pulled out a tube of KY jelly. This time silence and wide eyes of disbelief – I was losing them, I could feel it.

"I may not touch the other body with my hands, but may" – and here I took hold of the penis – "direct this lubricated appendage towards its goal."

I could have heard a pin drop, but no pin dropped. Everyone was stock-still.

"The winner," I continued, "will be the first couple to make a cock come."

I fell silent. A deathly hush for five seconds or more, but I kept my composure.

Then Lady Hesketh – who, together with her partner, the Japanese consulate's daughter, had put in the second highest bid – started to clap.

"Bravo!" she shouted. "Bravo!"

The others followed suit, clapping and shouting their approval for my bold move.

"Thank you ladies and 'gentlemen,'" I said, with a bow that made my penis wobble. "And now I ask the other contestants to equip themselves and take up positions."

Eleven other couples opened their cabinets and took out feather dusters, flails and dildos. Mine was the only white phallus, the rest were black, but otherwise of the same size and design. Lady Hesketh had trouble squeezing into her pants, but once in place her big dick looked very fetching and somehow appropriate for such a large and forceful woman. Beside her, Minako, the Japanese consul's daughter, seemed small and fragile in her pink satin frock, but together they were to prove a formidable team.

I stepped forward and surveyed the row: eleven penises present, correct and upstanding; eleven right hands with leather flails, and eleven left hands with feather dusters, present, correct and ready to go. I glanced at the monitors. The men were snoozing, perhaps dreaming of what they would do with their $3,000, hoping this job would soon be done and that they would be released from their prisons. They had no idea what lay in store, and, again, I felt a thrill of excitement at the thought of twelve faces suddenly registering a double dose of sexual interference below.

"On the count of three, ladies and gentlemen, you may begin," I said into the microphone. "And may the best pair win. One, two, three! Go!"

The couples scrambled on to the plinths, took up positions fore and aft and then seemed to lose their nerve.

Some turned to see what I would do, others stared at the cocks and bottoms unable to move. I prepared to start the action, but was beaten to it by Lady Hesketh. With a roar she grabbed her penis, smeared it with jelly and rammed it up Batman. The face on the second screen screamed in pain. You could not hear the scream, but you could see it. Eyes wide, mouth open. Minako, taking her cue, lifted the flail and began to whip the poor man's cock, a grin spreading across her delicate Japanese features as she did so. She was not as demure as her pink frock suggested, and a dab hand at flailing. But on checking Batman's groin screen, I saw that, despite their efforts, response was minimal.

I decided to take a more gentle approach with Superman. I told Mona to start dusting while I greased my dildo. When her feathers touched his cock, the face on screen one registered surprise, but then smiled, buttocks on screen three clenched in pleasure and, on screen two, the cock itself uncurled and lifted into the air. Mona continued to dust deftly, and the more she did so, the more our cock crowed. I took hold of my white dildo and moved it towards the brown buttocks protruding from Superman's behind. I longed to reach out and squeeze them, but rules were rules and I had to set an example. I let my penis hover an inch from the crack and waited. Mona seemed to be doing all right on her own and I did not want to upset the applecart by intervening too soon.

I glanced down the other monitors.

Hesketh and Minako were still going at it hammer and tongs with Hesketh's bottom on screen three bouncing up and down in time to Batman's balls on screen two. The face on screen one shed tears, but neither Hesketh nor Minako seemed concerned, or aware that there was a face. They concentrated on flesh below, and Minako, flailing hard, appeared to be approaching orgasm herself. Further down, the Chief Secretary's daughter was having success with the lad inside Mick Jagger. She had inserted her dildo up his behind, but was now content to hold it there, quite still, while her partner – an unknown lady in turquoise – flailed the balls with her flail and tickled the cock with her duster. The face was enjoying it, the cock responding well, so I would have to keep an eye on them.

I returned to Superman. His cock was fully extended and Mona was tickling it more fiercely, as well as massaging his balls with the leather handle of her flail. The time had come to make an entrance.

I parted the buttocks with the tip of my dildo and searched for the anus. The face registered fear, the cock wilted. I withdrew. Mona recovered the situation and I tried again. This time the face pursed its lips, closed its eyes and let me enter. I felt my dildo slip inside and watched with satisfaction as my man's lips on screen one opened to receive the mouth of the girlfriend or boyfriend in his mind's eye. I felt the near end of the dildo push against my clitoris. I rotated my pelvis and watched the dildo churn inside my boy. His tongue slipped out and his eyes closed tighter. His cock on screen two stretched out towards Mona like an ostrich at feeding time, the hole at its tip opening up like a mollusc's mouth. I began to move my penis in and out, gradually increasing speed and intensity, while keeping one eye on the screens above. And as his pleasure increased, so did my own, and as his cock distended to bursting point, so my own body neared climax.

Further down, I saw Jagger about to ejaculate.

I closed my eyes and thrust, as hard as I could, deep into the anus of my brown-bottomed Superman, feeling the dildo squeeze and squash my clitoris as it reached and probed his prostate. I opened my eyes wide and gave a shriek of pleasure and, as I did so, I saw a white fountain burst from the mollusc's mouth and shoot towards Mona, who jumped back in alarm and then raised her arms in triumph.

Our man had come, I had come and we had won.

Shortly afterwards, the lad inside Jagger came, then, in quick succession, the boys inside Chan, Cruise and Beckham – only poor old Batman was as limp at the end as he had been at the start. I felt sorry for Lord Hesketh, and hoped Minako's husband was a fan of the flail. But the evening had been a success and, after dismantling dildos, downing dusters and recalling the Tibetan girls to remove and empty the installations, the band returned and we danced and pranced into the small hours. A night to remember, a night worth three million dollars in scholarships, and I went home a proud and satisfied woman, glad to have, yet again, done my bit for charity.

And now – as I sit here on the Peak, in the peace and quiet of my own garden, with the breeze rippling the pool, the songbirds preparing for bed in the bamboo grove and a glorious sunset settling over the South China Sea to the West – I say to myself: the world's not such a bad place after all. I say to myself: what a wonderful world!

THE TERRORISTS

She waited on the opposite side of the road, hidden in the undergrowth beneath the walkway that leads from the gardens of the Hong Kong Academy for Performing Arts to the shopping mall at Pacific Place.

The men trickled out of a heavily guarded gate on the far side of a two-lane highway – or more precisely waddled out. They appeared in pairs, or in groups of three or four, but never alone 'for security reasons,' and never more than five at a time so as not to 'intimidate the local population.' Tall, small, black, brown, beige and white men – all overfed and under exercised. Out they waddled into the midday sun, surveyed their surroundings and set off in baggy shorts and knee-length T-shirts, or skin-tight jeans and fresh-pressed chinos, to spend their dollars and 'do their thing.'

USS *Invincible* – the world's longest, fattest, largest aircraft carrier – had dropped anchor near Hong Kong and was now spewing out its three thousand occupants in relays and bussing them by boat to Fenwick Pier at the Fleet Arcade on Harbour Road, just a stone's throw from the Tamar barracks of the People's Liberation Army and the prostitutes of Wanchai. Blue and white double-decker boat-buses ploughing back and forth, delivering fifty sailors every fifteen minutes day-in, day-out for three days – an invasion of flab and excess, an overrunning of Hong Kong by brainwashed and washed out sailors ordered to 'take care, be polite and have fun.' Twenty-four hours of R&R for America's finest, America's un-fittest, America's fine-tuned killing machine; the men – and odd woman – who serviced the planes that carried the bombs that killed the people that stood in the way of American foreign policy goals.

Defending liberty, Ma'am! Keeping the peace, Sir!

Not in the view of the woman watching. More like a band of thugs, a tribe of overpaid terrorists, forcing the values of a corrupt and bloated American Democracy on to anyone who did not dance to their tune. Overfed animals immune to prosecution, immune to the suffering they caused. It made her sick, this tri-annual flexing of American muscle, this disgorging of American manpower into the heart of Hong Kong. But it also gave her a chance, and she took it every time: 'Less they forget, less she forget.' As a child, she, too, had welcomed the sailors in her hometown, not knowing then what she knew now: running after them, begging them for coins or cigarettes or candies, and then, when older, flashing her eyes and wiggling her hips – even once kissing a tall, handsome black man on the lips. Until she learnt the truth, that is, and then she stopped.

Now she watched and waited, stock-still behind her Bauhinia bush. If one particular man caught her eye, she used her mobile phone to prompt a colleague across the road, who then approached the named party and handed him a leaflet with directions to a bar in Wanchai. Usually the ones pinpointed were the healthier-looking white men. These were the junior officers, a superior class of sailor, rarely black and rarely overweight. It was one of these who, twenty-five years before, had raped her mother outside Subic Bay in the Philippines and left his seaman's semen to turn into her, Gloria Ramos, the woman hidden in the undergrowth with a mobile phone; the woman watching with sunglasses perched in her long black hair and eyes peeled for suitable prey.

Gloria was a member of a group called Sex Workers Against American Terror, or SWAAT for short. It was made up of women who had experienced – directly, or indirectly through a relative – American military intervention in a close-up and unpleasant way. From Korea to Kuwait, from the Philippines to Panama, from Kosovo to Okinawa, Vietnam and Cambodia – wherever American servicemen had been stationed, or even just visited – there were victims of murder, rape and sexual abuse; some as young as twelve, some already married to local husbands, some no longer alive to tell their tale. In Hong Kong, there were eight SWAAT members working in two teams of four. In Gloria's team, there was an

Indonesian called Maya, who had been forced to have oral sex with three American soldiers when working as a maid in Singapore; Pak-san, a ground staff employee of Korean Air, whose twelve-year-old sister had been abused and beaten to death in a Seoul back street by two US marines; and Anna, a forty-year-old from Kosovo, whose eighteen-year-old daughter had been murdered by an American military policeman for refusing to go to bed with him. Of these, Anna was the most militant, and it was all Gloria could do to restrain her from attacking the sailors on the street or hurling a petrol bomb into the crowded interior of their favourite haunt – Joe Banana's, in Wanchai.

It was a Sunday around two in the afternoon and the space behind Gloria's hiding place had filled up with Filipino maids singing hymns, eating vinegar-soaked chicken or practicing their synchronized dance routines. Her presence in the bushes was unnoticed and unremarkable. Every available nook and cranny, from concrete stairwells to cramped corners beneath noisy flyovers, was filled with Filipinos at this time on the Lord's Day of Rest. Not that Gloria looked, or even acted, like a Filipino. She was six-foot-tall and Western in appearance: dark Spanish hair; long, well-proportioned legs; a trim waist; round, inviting buttocks; firm, protruding breasts; and an elegant, aquiline nose much larger than those of her full-blooded sisters. Only her powerful, black eyes gave a hint of East Asian ancestry and it was these – along with her Playboy figure and familiar Western mannerisms – that she used to lure pupils into school.

Despite being born the illegitimate child of a cleaning lady in the former American base of Subic Bay, she had managed to make good and break the illiteracy mould of generations. After a hungry but happy early childhood with her grandmother in Pangasinan, she had returned to live with her mother in Subic's suburbs and, on hearing the truth about her conception, sublimated her anger and disgust in long hours of night time study. At the age of eighteen, she won a place at law school in Manila and spent the next four years improving her mind and learning the social mores and behavioural mannerisms of the better off and better educated. By the time she graduated, she could speak perfect English, eat dinner at an expensive restaurant without putting a fork wrong and engage in intelligent conversation with people from much more exalted and moneyed backgrounds than her own. She also had a Bachelor of Law degree and was soon taken on as a trainee paralegal by a downtown firm of lawyers. But this was the Philippines, not New York, and her pay amounted to little more than seven thousand pesos a month, or less than a third of what her village friends from Pangasinan were now earning as maids in Hong Kong. So, under pressure from her mother – who had helped pay the college fees and was now suffering from arthritis – Gloria agreed to drop her legal career for five years and become a 'foreign domestic' in Hong Kong.

For the first two years, she worked as a live-in maid. Then, just before her first contract was due to expire, she discovered Anna. Anna had married a British policeman sent to Kosovo to train a new law enforcement agency. He had not only offered the grieving mother a sympathetic ear and two broad shoulders to cry on, but also undertaken his own investigation into her daughter's death, uncovered the murderer's identity and started proceedings. The US military ignored the evidence and refused to extradite the officer, but Anna fell head over heels in love with her British 'bobby.' They married and moved to Hong Kong, where her husband had landed a senior job in the post-handover police force and where Anna was happy to play housewife in a Repulse Bay apartment. Gloria had answered an advertisement placed by Anna in the Wanchai Park n' Shop and the two hit it off. While Gloria cleaned, they talked and soon knew everything about each other, including their shared hatred of the US military's abuse of women. Anna persuaded her husband to sign a fulltime contract for Gloria, but told her new friend she only had to clean twice a week. This meant Gloria was legal in Hong Kong without being tied to twenty-four hour live-in service, and, occasionally, she topped up her income with work as a high-class escort, offering dinner, dancing and massage, but no intercourse or kissing. She charged two thousand HK for an evening and if, during dinner, she took a dislike to the client, she 'disappeared,' leaving the man with the bill and a dent in his ego.

It was through this work that she met Pak-san – the woman distributing leaflets across the road – and Maya. Maya was half-hotel maid, half-pole dancer. She had founded the Hong Kong section of SWAAT and, together with Pak-san, had carried out several operations on lower ranked US sailors. Pak-san was Maya's lover and herself an occasional sex worker – of sorts. She augmented her airline income by dressing up in men's clothes and entertaining Japanese wives at a Shinjuku-style club in North Point. Though the tips she received were generous, she regarded her activity as a more moral form of sex work than priming a rich man's penis. Japanese husbands mistreated their wives and she brought a little love into empty lives. Maya dismissed this positive spin on her lover's lesbian prostitution and said Pak-san was just after 'Japanese pussy.' Pak-san then sulked and Gloria had to mediate before attention could be refocused on the SWAAT business in hand. In fact, it was this ability to calm and control that led to Gloria's nomination as cell leader. She had accepted the role on condition that Anna – not a sex worker – be allowed to join. Maya did not trust people outside the trade, but Pak-san was keen to have an older woman involved, so Anna joined and Gloria took command.

Today's outing was her first re-education project as leader, and she wanted no slip-ups.

She told Pak-san to continue leafleting for ten minutes and then head to Lockhart Road. She closed her mobile phone, lowered her Calvin Klein sunglasses and emerged from the bushes. She crossed Gloucester Road by way of the Harcourt Gardens pedestrian bridge, doubled back past police headquarters and turned up Arsenal Street towards Jaffe Road and the ex-pat drinking holes. She wanted to assess the sailors' mood. Were they tense, wary and on edge, or relaxed and ready to let rip?

She turned left into Jaffe Road and saw a huddle of men – three black and two white – outside the Wanch music bar. As she approached, the men sized her up and began that kind of inane male giggle and body jiggle intended to display disdain and interest at the same time. Gloria let their eyes roam over her six-foot frame, taut white blouse, skin-tight leather pants and high-heeled boots, and passed by on the far side of the road.

"Want a drink, lady?" one of the white boys shouted.

"Not with you, boy," a black sailor guffawed. "She's after a real man!"

The other black sailors clapped their friend on the back and headed into the Wanch. The white boy gazed after Gloria watching her behind rise and fall.

"That's one hell of an ass!" he called out in imitation of the black man's accent.

Gloria turned and stared at the two white boys – pasty faces, long shorts, baggy T-shirts, baseball caps. Not long out of school, she thought, recruited from some white ghetto with no other jobs and then press-ganged into service to keep them off the streets.

The admirer's friend caught her eye, turned red and tugged at his colleague's arm.

"Come on, Shorty! She's too much for you."

Gloria felt sorry for them. They seemed so vulnerable: their bravado an act required of sailors; their need for love and warmth denied by the traditions of military machismo; their real selves lost in crewcuts and alcohol. She wanted to give them a motherly hug, or perhaps a sisterly hug, as any one of them could be her brother. Despite her hatred of the American military, she did not hate the individual men – certainly not in the lower ranks. They were victims, too – like her, like all hard-up people from Hong Kong to Harlem. They were all forced into slavery for the rich and powerful – as maids, as servicemen, as members of the keep-your-mouth shut and do-as-you're-told majority.

"Have a good time, boys!" she shouted. "And be nice to the girls!"

"Yes, ma'am!" they called back. "Have a nice day."

She gave them an extra wiggle and walked on. They were not her prey, but did seem relaxed and at ease – no red alert surrounding this R&R, no high 'terrorist threat' rating for Hong Kong.

In a bedsit in Lockhart Street, she met up with Pak-san, who was now wearing her Korean Airlines ground-staff uniform.

"Ready for duty, ma'am!" she said, standing to attention in front of Gloria.

"Why the uniform, Pak?"

"Ten per cent discount for airline staff, ma'am"

"At the Grand Hyatt?"

"Just this week. They think air hostesses will attract more US officers!"

Gloria laughed and surveyed the room: double bed, lopsided wardrobe, minuscule dining table, cardboard box stuffed with pole-dancing thongs, spare Grand Hyatt housekeeping uniform hanging behind the door. She wondered how Pak-san and Maya managed to survive. They must be in love to put up with a rabbit hutch like this.

"Maya at work?"

"Yes, ma'am!"

"And the other team ready to go in Laguna?"

"Yes, ma'am. All leaflets distributed as per your orders, ma'am."

"Stop calling me 'ma'am,' Pak – we're not in the army."

"Yes, ma'am. It's just your leather pants, ma'am. They're so butch and sexy!"

Gloria tried to grab Pak-san, but the Korean's wiry, five-foot frame was already out of the door – overnight bag on one shoulder, camcorder on the other.

"And no flirting with the chambermaids!" Gloria shouted. "I want you ready and waiting when I call, not sharing a shower with some housekeeping whore."

"No, ma'am!"

Gloria slumped in a chair and closed her eyes. Pak-san ogled anything with a fanny, but remained faithful to Maya and meticulous in her execution of SWAAT duties. The plan today was complex and required patience and persistence. The centre of operations was the Grand Hyatt. Maya was already there in her role as a chambermaid and Pak-san on her way to check in. Gloria had checked in earlier with Anna, who was 'officially' attending an art fair at the Exhibition Centre, and had told her husband she needed a hotel room to discuss purchases. Her husband, a trusting man, had agreed to pay for two nights at the Grand Hyatt, but, to avoid causing difficulties for him should anything go wrong, had not been told his wife would share the room with Gloria.

Not that anything would go wrong, Gloria assured herself, as, half an hour later, she applied lipstick in Maya's tiny shower cubicle.

All she had to do was find a couple of American officers and seduce them into a threesome. Seduce them without evoking the slightest suspicion in their paranoid military minds. A challenge, but one she was up to.

She strolled to the Grand Hyatt by way of a walkway connecting Wanchai MTR to the Convention Centre. The day was hot and sticky and the route maximized air-con. After passing through the gold-leaved lobby of the New World Centre, she crossed a bridge and entered the reception area of the Harbour View Hotel. Sailors were checking in, or standing in clusters ready for the off to Wanchai. Eyes turned as her body cast its spell. Only those partnered with female crew, or committed to wives and girlfriends flown in for the weekend, ignored the curves. Most clocked the goods and mentally undressed her six-foot frame as she crossed to the lift lobby. She took a lift to the eleventh floor garden shared with the grander Grand Hyatt, flashed her room card at the entrance and indicated she was passing through and not in need of a towel. If Anna had done her homework, the guys would be earmarked. All Gloria had to do was reel them in.

"Get your sexiest bikini on and go!" was Anna's comment as Gloria entered their fifteenth-floor room.

"Let's see," Gloria said, joining Anna at the window and grabbing the high-powered binoculars from her friend's hand.

The room had a bird's eye view of the pool area and, as she focused up the lenses, a sea of half-naked bodies came into view

"Five in the Jacuzzi," Anna whispered in her Balkan accent. "I watched them arrive in the lobby. All officers, all arrogant bastards!"

"How do you know?"

"They do not let me into lift first. And then, when in lift, they take no notice of beautiful, middle-aged woman beside them."

"What floor?" Gloria asked, ignoring Anna's hurt pride.

"Eighteenth and nineteenth. Single rooms, but all buddies, I would say."

"Good," nodded Gloria, lowering the binoculars and handing them to Anna.

She crossed to the bed, removed her blouse, leather trousers, bra and panties and selected a white, wet-look bikini from her suitcase.

"Perfect," Anna sighed.

Gloria glanced up and saw the binoculars were now trained on her naked breasts.

"Anna!"

"I'm so jealous, Gloria. You have such a marvellous body."

"And so do you," soothed Gloria, pulling up the high-backed bikini bottoms until the rear thong lodged tightly between her buttocks.

"You think so?" sighed Anna again, smoothing down the pleats of her beige linen dress and checking the bun at the back of her fiery red hair.

She was a plump woman, but still attractive, and her face, despite wrinkles and double chin, exuded a dignity and determination that allowed her to mingle naturally with the Grand Hyatt's up-market clientele when on active duty for SWAAT.

"You really think so?"

"Of course," laughed Gloria, fastening the top of her bikini and positioning her breasts for maximum effect. "You hooked a top British bobby, didn't you?"

"With a big nose and a beer belly, yes!"

"He's sweet."

"Yes. But you…"

"Come on, Anna," interrupted Gloria, pulling on her bathrobe. "Time for work."

Anna repositioned herself at the window, binoculars trained on the prey.

"When I lie back with hands behind my head, you call," continued Gloria, tucking her mobile into a Donna Karan bag and dabbing Toko Furumi on to her wrists and neck.

"Good luck," said Anna, giving her maid, friend and comrade a kiss. "Be careful."

"This is the easy bit!" chuckled Gloria. "Bye."

A few minutes later, she emerged poolside.

An attendant, in short-sleeved shirt and steam-pressed shorts, showed her to a lounger near the refreshment bar. She ignored him and headed for a vacant space by the Jacuzzi. The attendant hurried after her with a set of towels and laid them out on the chosen chair. She thanked him, ordered a Campari on ice with a dash of vodka and stood surveying the scene. Still in her white towelling bathrobe, she drew little attention from the five men, half submerged with their beer cans in the bubbling water.

Then, with a swirl, she unwrapped the robe, slipped it off her shoulders and bent to place it beneath the sun bed. Her barely covered bottom and long legs were now only inches from the men in the Jacuzzi. She felt their eyes hit her and their breathing stop.

"Butt to starboard and it's mine!" hissed one of the men in a stage whisper.

They were drunk, or nearly so, unconcerned at being overheard.

"Get a load of that," commented another.

Gloria straightened up and turned to lie down on the sun bed, making sure the men caught a good glimpse of her face, breasts and crotch as she did so.

"Wow! A looker, too!" a third man added, putting a camera to his eye.

The camera flashed, she flashed a smile in return and lay down.

"With boobies to match," put in a fourth, also in a stage whisper.

"They're mine," said a fifth.

"Over my dead body!" said the first.

There was the sound of someone being ducked and gasping for breath, followed by the clapping of hands and a round of bawdy male laughter. An attendant ran across and asked the men to keep their voices down.

Gloria lay back and surveyed the Jacuzzi from the corner of her eye. She wanted two of them. Not all five, and not just one. Two. This was where luck came in, combined with the female trapper's skill. The men continued to eye her up and exchange stage whispers. By a process of elimination, she identified the two who had claimed ownership over her body. One was a twenty-something blonde with a smooth chest and well-muscled arms, the other was pushing forty with dark hair on his head and torso, and the beginnings of a bald patch. They were trim-figured, with healthy complexions and educated voices – all hallmarks of the officer-class.

When her drink arrived, she sat up, raised her backrest and gave the two men a significant smile each, ignoring the efforts of the man with the camera – a bull-necked oaf with thick thighs and ginger hair – to attract her attention for another snap. She felt like a cowhand sorting the best-hung bulls. No lasso. Just looks. After five minutes, the chosen cattle conferred, ordered more beers and emerged dripping from the far side of the Jacuzzi. They hesitated and then padded over to Gloria, water streaming down their bodies, bulges bulging behind brief swimming trunks.

"Mind if we join you, ma'am?" the blonde asked in a polite, well-practiced tone of voice.

"Be my guest!" replied Gloria, taking a sip of Campari.

Her shades were on, protecting her eyes from the afternoon sun and allowing undetected observation of the haul.

The two men lowered themselves on to a neighbouring lounger.

"Kent," said the blonde, putting out a hand.

Gloria nodded, but did not take the hand.

"And this is Mike," Kent added, indicating his swarthier colleague.

"Belinda," Gloria said with a smile, and then, taking another sip of Campari, she leant back and closed her eyes. She would let them make the moves.

"We had this bet see, Belinda," Kent began again. "I said you were Mexican. But Mike said – after you'd removed the robe – you had to be Brazilian."

"After I'd removed the robe?" Gloria inquired without opening her eyes.

"Well, Belinda," Mike said, speaking for the first time, "and I mean this as a complement, you've got one hell of a figure. I've only seen curves that good in Rio."

"Thank you, Mike," Gloria replied with a smile. "Yours aren't bad, either."

Mike blushed and pulled in his already taut stomach. Kent laughed.

"How do you boys manage to keep so trim?" Gloria continued.

"We're in the navy," Kent replied – as if that were answer enough.

"Oh!" exclaimed Gloria. "From that aircraft carrier on the news? The *Impetuous*."

"*Invincible*," said Mike with pride. "Two all-American sailors at your service!"

Kent dug him in the ribs.

"Ignore him, Belinda. He's just got promotion."

"Congratulations," said Gloria. She raised her sunglasses and let her eyes dart back and forth between the two men. "Seems like you guys all hang out in pairs. I noticed on the waterfront this morning. Is that a regulation thing?"

Kent leant forward.

"Security measure," he whispered.

"At all times?" Gloria asked, a twinkle in her eye.

"Strictly speaking, yes, ma'am," Mike said, taking a swig from his can of beer.

"Even when…" she egged them on.

"Regulations state shore buddies should not indulge in unaccompanied activity," Kent chipped in.

"Which means one of them has to wait outside the door while the other does it," concluded Mike, draining his can in one and grinning.

"Mike!" exclaimed Kent.

"Unless the lady likes two at a time," Gloria said, replacing her sunglasses

She watched from behind the polarized glass, waiting for her remark to sink in. Kent nudged Mike. Mike nudged him back. Kent took a deep breath.

"You into that, ma'am? If you don't mind me asking?"

Gloria summoned the waiter. Kent and Mike looked nervous. Was she going to complain? Had they gone too far? The waiter arrived. Gloria ordered a top-up. When the waiter was gone, she raised her knees and smiled.

"I'd prefer it to someone eavesdropping at my door."

The two officers were confused by this reply, not sure if she was saying yes or making a general observation. They laughed politely. Mike drained his already-empty can. Kent stared at his toes. Gloria let them sweat and then put her hands behind her head.

"You boys want to join me for dinner tonight?"

"Both of us?" exclaimed Kent and Mike together.

"Why not," replied Gloria, as her mobile started to ring. "Shall we say eight o'clock in Grissini's, on the eighth floor? You like Italian food?"

"Yes, ma'am," they replied.

Gloria answered the phone and listened for a moment.

"Right," she muttered. "I'll be straight over." She closed the phone, slipped off the sun-bed and stood up. "Sorry, boys. Duty calls."

"If you don't mind me asking," Kent said, as he helped her on with her robe. "What do you do for a living?"

"I'm a lawyer," Gloria replied, fastening the towelling tie around her waist and striding off towards the hotel.

"From Brazil?" Mike called out.

"Tell you, tonight," Gloria shouted back. "At eight."

An hour later, at five o'clock, the SWAAT team met in Anna's room to finalise plans.

Maya, a twenty-five-year-old Sumatran of medium build, sat on the edge of the bed in her housekeeping uniform; her black hair tied in a ponytail, her makeup discreet in line with hotel regulations. Pak-san, still in KAL uniform, lay across the foot of the bed. Gloria, in bathrobe, and Anna, in beige linen dress, sat at a mahogany table by the window ticking off items on a checklist. The team divided into four areas of expertise – the S&M's, as Gloria called them: seduction, surveillance, medicine and money. Anna bankrolled the operations; Maya – a trained nurse who, like Gloria, had found she could earn more as a maid in Hong Kong than as a hospital worker in Indonesia – administered medication to uncooperative officers; Pak-san – a black-belt judo expert with a degree in Communications from Seoul University – ran the post and pre-op surveillance elements, including video recording and computer hacking when needed; and Gloria selected and pulled in the male fish for neo-feminist filleting by the team as a whole. She also used her legal mind to fine-tune strategy and check for obvious blunders in the game plan.

"The action must be in this room, not theirs," she was saying. "Or we lose access for the team. Anna, make sure your gear is hidden. No stockings in the bathroom or panties under the pillow."

Anna nodded and made a note on the piece of paper in front of her.

"What if they check cupboards before you've got 'em stripped?" Pak-san asked, without moving from her horizontal position on the bed. "You said they were paranoid."

"They are, but they won't," Anna replied. "One man will check. Two do not bother. Too confident."

"Which is why Maya must be outside the door with a master key dead on time!" Gloria added. "I want the knock-out drop administered before they get to work on me."

"Pak and Anna will do that," remarked Maya in a disgruntled tone.

"You've given them the anaesthetic pads?"

"Yes," muttered Maya. "In fact, you don't really need me at all."

"Maya!" Gloria said, crossing over to give the Indonesian a hug. "Of course we need you. Once pacified, the men's vital functions must be monitored while we take photographs and secure them for retraining. We don't want corpses."

"More's the pity," snorted Anna.

"Anna!" Gloria hissed. "You know the rules."

Anna made a mock karate chop, but nodded.

"And don't hold the pad on too long!" Maya warned, glancing at Pak and Anna.

"all right on a single-handed double-arm twist, Anna?" Pak-san called out.

"I can do a double-handed single-ball twist," laughed Anna. "Make them squeal like pigs."

"You'd be a dead pig before you heard them squeal," Pak-san said, rolling on to her stomach and firing a finger at Anna. "They're trained to respond in seconds. Grabbing balls does not disarm hands. Understood?"

"Yes, Captain Pak," Anna said, giving a mock salute.

"And Gloria?" Pak-san added, turning to the team leader.

"What is it, Pak?" Gloria replied, glancing across at the impish face with its henna-tinted, short cut-hair and beady black eyes staring at her from the bed.

"You'll have to keep them fully distracted."

"I know."

"Which means you'll have to let them almost…"

"Start?"

Pak-san nodded.

"I know," Gloria said. "One with his back to the wardrobe, where Anna is hiding, and one with his back to the bathroom, where you will emerge from the ceiling space."

Pak-san nodded. There was silence in the room. Then Maya put up her hand.

"What if they don't want oral and normal?"

"What do you mean?" Pak-san asked.

"What if they want these two holes," she said, pointing between her legs. "That's usually done lying down, isn't it?"

Pak-san and Anna burst out laughing. Maya blushed and fingered the hem of her uniform. Gloria's expression remained serious.

"Maya is right. We must think of everything. Men are unpredictable and often violent. But I am big and they will do as I ask – at the start. Do you trust me, Maya?"

Maya nodded and looked at her watch.

"I must go. I've been too long on this room. See you at ten thirty!"

She bent to kiss Pak-san and then slipped out of the door with her cleaning trolley. Pak-san knelt on the bed and began thrusting her hips back and forth.

"Try me, Anna. One, two, three…"

Anna pounced from the table, twisted Pak-san's arms up behind her back, locked them in position with one hand and then jammed a free palm over the Korean's mouth.

"Excellent!" exclaimed Gloria. "I have nothing to fear."

Four hours later, at ten o'clock, Gloria, Kent and Mike were coming to the end of their meal in Grissini's Italian Restaurant on the eighth floor of the Grand Hyatt Hotel.

They were seated beside a floor-to-ceiling window overlooking Victoria Harbour and the neon-lit skyline of Hong Kong Island's Central district. Gloria had positioned herself between the two men and was wearing a white linen suit with short pleated skirt and embroidered jacket, a low-cut cream satin top, pale silk stockings and five-inch heels. Her hair was piled up on top of her head in the 'organised chaos' style of the moment and she looked every bit the glamorous, educated and well-off lawyer she claimed to be. She had ordered a simple steamed 'pesci' dish with asparagus tips and sun-dried tomatoes on the side, and a single glass of Chianti to settle her nerves. That was all. The men – both dressed in blue blazers, open necked white shirts and loose fitting chinos – had eaten mounds of pasta for starters, followed up with steaks, broccoli and fried potatoes, and rounded things off with a tiramisu apiece. A bottle and a half of house Lambrusco had washed this mountain down and they were now merry, staring at Gloria's breasts and no longer listening to her ruby red lips.

"You boys full?" she said, wiping her mouth with the napkin from her lap.

"Sure are, Belinda!" said Kent, raising his glass. "Here's to your excellent choice of restaurant…"

"And your excellent choice of clothing," chimed in Mike, who was the drunker of the two and less reticent than by the pool. "You look stunning! Wow!"

She felt a hand reach under the table for her thigh and gently repelled it.

"Later, Mike!" she whispered. "I've a reputation as a lawyer to maintain."

"You can defend us anytime, ma'am," Mike said. "Ain't that right, Kent?"

"Sure is."

The men were ready for action. Any more delay and they would start looking at other dates – any more drink and they would be out of it. Gloria glanced at her watch. She had twenty minutes to get them undressed and in position.

"Shall we order coffee upstairs?" she said. "Maybe work off the food first?"

The men winked at each other, keen to sow a few American oats in the fertile furrows of a broad-beamed Brazilian lawyer, happy to spread her legs and teach her the meaning of US democracy.

Gloria called over the waiter and charged the bill to her room. She did not want the men to think she was on the sponge, or a hooker in disguise. Picking up the tab gave her credibility, kept her in control. She slid a hundred dollar tip under her wineglass and rose to leave. The men's eyes followed her and Mike whistled between his teeth.

"Top or bottom?" she heard him whisper to Kent.

"Turn and turn about," was the sniggered reply.

Gloria hoped the team was in position. These naval officers were big men with big appetites. She did not want their perverted fantasies let loose on her, or any other girl, until they had learnt to temper testosterone with tenderness.

When they reached the lift, Gloria entered first. The men followed, but, as she put her finger on the fifteenth floor button, Mike removed it.

"Might be cosier at our place, Belinda," he said, selecting the thirty-sixth floor with one hand and her behind with the other.

"But we agreed," protested Gloria, trying to remove the groping fingers and wondering why he had picked a floor where neither man was staying.

"Your place, our place? What's the odds?" drawled Kent, as he ran the index finger of his right hand down her cheek.

"I need to prepare…" began Gloria.

"What?" barked Mike, thrusting a hand between her legs from behind and gripping the gusset of her panties. "You've all we need, right here – Gloria!"

Gloria froze. How did they know her name? Had they uncovered the whole plot? Had Anna, Pak-san and Maya been rounded up and spirited away onto the carrier? Stay calm. See how much they know before hitting the panic button.

"Belinda's my name," she said, as Mike tightened his grip on the panties and put a tongue in her ear. "And I don't like being manhandled. I am a trained lawyer…"

"From the Philippines," hissed Mike.

"Currently working as a maid in Hong Kong," added Kent.

"And moonlighting as an escort for businessmen and diplomats," concluded Mike.

Shit! They'd done a check, but how? Her mind raced. She had been with an American diplomat, a month ago. An ugly bastard

148

who wanted to beat her. She'd vamoosed after dinner, leaving him to settle up. Was he the source?

"Got you taped, eh?" Kent grinned, his mouth too close to hers.

She remained silent. Mike's hand was still clamped between her legs, Kent blocking her to the front. She needed to think.

"Want to know how we know?" added Kent, putting a hand under her jacket and round her left breast.

"Want to know?" repeated Mike, yanking the gusset of her panties back so that it dug into her vulva.

The lift was passing the twenty-sixth floor, ten floors to go. Better check what they knew and then make a run for it. She had seen off two men before.

"Spill the beans," she said, pretending to be bored by the men's groping hands.

"Sent that picture from the pool over to consulate security," Mike said.

"And security found a match in one of our agent's photo albums!" continued Kent, massaging her left nipple through the satin of her blouse.

Shit again!

The fat guy had got a waiter to snap them over champagne. She remembered now – chubby arm round her shoulder and 'say cheese for the camera.' She should have been more careful, and by the pool earlier. But how did you turn down an innocent request for a snapshot without seeming mean or raising suspicions?

"Which was checked against Hong Kong Immigration records," concluded Mike. "Jigsaw complete."

He released her panties. The lift reached the thirty-sixth floor. Gloria waited for the doors to open.

"Look guys," she sighed. "You've rumbled me. I'm not a Brazilian lawyer – just a high-class whore. So let's part friends."

She put out a finger to press the fifteenth-floor button. Again, Mike's hand prevented her from doing so. Kent held the doors open with his foot.

"We don't mind a Filipino whore," said Mike, tightening his hold on her wrist.

"Not with a figure like this one!" chortled Kent.

"I'd rather not…" began Gloria.

Mike leant in close.

"Want your employer to know about those after-hours antics?"

Gloria froze. Did they know about Anna? Had they been following her, too?

"He's a top cop, and top cops don't like moonlighters," Kent added.

Gloria gave an inner sigh of relief. Of course! It was Anna's husband who signed the contract, not Anna. And the contract filed at Immigration was as far as the two men's trail led – a contract telling them her employer was an upstanding Hong Kong resident employing a Filipino maid. Nothing more.

Gloria smiled at the men.

"OK," she said, shaking off Mike's hand and leaving the lift of her own accord. "You win. But I only do massage."

The two men glanced at each other and winked.

"That's cool," Kent said. "A hand job in Hong Kong. That's cool."

Mike led the way down the carpeted corridor to a door at the far end.

Gloria made her plan.

The men were relaxed again, sure of their prey. They assumed the threat of disclosure would keep her docile and felt no need to use restraint. That was important. Her body was free for fast and effective action at an appropriate moment. She would let Mike open the bedroom door, push him inside, back-kick Kent in the balls as he moved to grab her and make an exit through the fire escape. She had seen off muggers in Manila, and that was before Pak-san's judo lessons. Handling two was well within her repertoire.

"Here we are," Mike said, as he reached the last door before the fire exit.

Gloria stood, waiting for him to take out a key. But he didn't. Instead the door opened and, before she knew it, Kent had pushed her through. Mike followed and slammed the door shut. She turned to face the two men – she could still handle them. But then, without warning, her arms were pinioned from behind. Her heart sunk.

Fear welled in her stomach. There was someone else in the room. She was outnumbered three to one.

"Remember me, babe?" a deep voice growled. "The photo-man at the pool?"

An image of the bull-necked oaf with ginger hair flashed through her mind.

"Todd the Butt Man, we call him," said Mike, taking off his blazer and unzipping his pants. "Mike the Mouth Man, that's me…"

"And Kent the Cunt Man!" chipped in Kent, unzipping his pants too.

"Three-way split we call it!" Todd added from behind. "It's what the new girls get when they join the ship. Kinda breaks them in!"

Gloria struggled, but her arms were pinioned – in the same way Anna and Pak would have pinioned the men for re-education – making any movement agony. She felt a hand lift the back of her skirt and grab her right buttock.

"An awesome ass!" whistled invisible Todd. "Am I gonna enjoy digging that!"

Gloria felt the man push his groin into her behind. He was already stripped to his shorts, ready for action. They must have planned this in the pool, after she had gone. So much for her strategic overview, so much for her ability to flush out flaws – she only hoped the SWAAT team could find her. But how? They knew where Mike and Kent's rooms were, but this Todd guy? He was in a penthouse suite judging by the floor number and the size of the room, a luxuriously appointed space boasting panoramic views of the harbour. Not a normal hangout for mid-ranking US naval officers and not somewhere Anna and the team would think of looking.

Must have private money, Gloria thought to herself, as she cursed her lack of foresight and wondered how to proceed.

But Todd moved first.

He jammed his free hand down the back of her panties and felt for her anus.

"Ouch!" she cried.

"Easy girl," Todd cooed. "We ain't started yet. Kent?"

Gloria watched as Kent, now down to his shorts, too, stepped forward, ripped open her jacket, tore off her top and pulled the peach satin bra she had bought earlier that day down to her waist. Three sets of drunken, lust-hardened eyes stared at her breasts — again the whistles, again Kent's clammy hand grabbing her nipples. She opened her mouth to scream, but thought better of it. No one would hear, and, even if they did, what was the word of a half-naked maid against three US officers, one with enough money to rent the presidential suite? Plus, she did not want them to make good on their threat to inform Anna's husband. Then Anna would be in trouble, too, and it was a golden SWAAT rule to limit damage. She would just have to wait. Keep her mouth shut and hope one of them left the room. Hope she could catch the other two off guard.

She felt Todd tie her wrists together behind her back with a towelling cord and then loop the end round her neck. She was being trussed like a turkey and her chances of escape were fading fast.

"Grab her legs!" Todd shouted, once the arms were secure.

"Yes, sir!"

Mike and Kent took a leg each and, together with Todd, manhandled her to a four-poster bed in the far corner of the room, where they lashed her — stomach down — to a dressing-table stool placed on the mattress. When they had finished, she had her wrists re-tied to the bed head and the rest of her body spread-eagled in a half-kneeling, half-lying position across the stool's seat — head and breasts hanging over its front end, groin and backside hovering above the mattress to the rear. Mike lifted her skirt and ripped off her panties. Kent splayed her legs and fastened her ankles to posts at the foot of the bed.

"Target vessel ready for attack, sir!" Kent yelled.

"Three-way split platoon ready for action, sir!" Mike sang out.

"Platoon! Prepare to board!" Todd commanded.

The three men dropped their underpants and grouped themselves around Gloria. Kent slipped his body between the legs of the footstool, until his groin was in position to enter her from beneath, and his mouth ready to grab her nipples. Mike knelt on the bed in front of the stool, his stubby penis pointing at Gloria's lips. Todd crouched between the splayed legs, his ginger-haired balls swaying above her naked behind.

"We're gonna fuck you three ways, Gloria," he said, grabbing hold of the neck cord and pulling her head back. "And if you resist, we're gonna fuck you some more!"

Gloria closed her eyes. Todd's forefinger probed her anus for a second time. Kent's hand fumbled with her vagina. Mike forced his thumb into her mouth.

Suddenly she saw her mother in the same situation. That was why her father had never been named. Mother had been gang-raped, but too ashamed to admit it. Pinned down and subjected to abuse in the darkness of a Subic Bay alley by a group of drunken officers, immune from prosecution and above the laws of the land they had 'liberated.' Gang-raped by the defenders of democracy – like her daughter now, in the penthouse suite of the Grand Hyatt Hotel, Hong Kong. Nothing had changed, except the location.

Gloria felt tears prick her eyes, but refused to cry.

"On a count of three," Todd yelled. "One, two…"

At that moment, the doorbell rang.

"Shit!" Mike exclaimed, his penis millimetres from Gloria's mouth.

"Ignore it," called up Kent from below. "I'm locked on target!"

"Me, too," shouted Todd, hands clamped on Gloria's behind.

Again the bell rang, and this time it was followed by the sound of a lock releasing.

"Shit!"

The door opened and a flash bulb lit up the room three times in quick succession.

"What the fuck?" yelled Todd.

The three men scrambled off the bed as the overhead light came on. Gloria peered over her shoulder. All she could see were two women in police uniform, one of them with a camera, accompanied by a housekeeping maid holding a master key card.

"Gentlemen!" a familiar voice barked. "You are under arrest! Sergeant Pak?"

The smaller of the two policewomen moved towards the naked men with four sets of handcuffs. Gloria could barely believe her eyes – the SWAAT team, in fancy dress.

"Whoa there!" called out Todd. "We're US Naval Officers…"

"I am aware of that," said Anna. "Secure the accused, Sergeant Pak."

"What's the charge?" protested Kent, his penis subsiding fast.

"Do I have to say?" barked Anna, pointing at Gloria with her superintendent's cane.

Where had she got that from, Gloria wondered – and the uniform?

"Just having fun," said Mike. "Weren't we, Gloria?"

"She's a hooker, see," added Todd. "Aren't you, Gloor?"

Gloria remained silent. Maya crossed to release her friend's bonds.

"Want us to tell your boss?" Todd threatened, moving back towards the bed.

But Pak grabbed his left arm, forced it up his spine and clipped on one end of a set of cuffs. She attached the other end to Mike's right wrist, clipped a second set to his left hand and connected this to Kent's right wrist. The third and fourth sets she used to lock the free arms, at either end of the chain gang, to the head and foot of the four-poster.

The three men now stood naked along the edge of the bed, unable to escape. Gloria climbed off the mattress, rubbed her wrists, flexed her neck and slipped into a bathrobe that Maya held open for her. She pulled up a chair in front of the officers.

"What the hell are you doing?" Todd yelled at Anna, as he tried in vain to break free from the bedpost.

"We have rights," whined Kent.

"Call our fleet commander!" said Mike.

Anna walked along the men slapping the cane against her calf-length police boots.

"Expecting US Cavalry?" she sneered, her accent thickening. "Invasion of Hong Kong to snatch you from hands of international justice? Like your government says it will do for US soldiers brought before Court of Human Rights in Holland?"

"We have our rights," repeated Kent, trying to cover his penis. "As US sailors…"

"And citizens!" added Mike.

"And, yeah," said Todd, yanking his hand up from Kent's groin, "they'll come and get us. You wait and see. America looks after its own…"

Anna shook her head and laughed.

"…And fucks the rest of us. Is that it?"

Todd went silent, and again started trying to free his wrist from the bedpost.

"What shall we do with them?" Anna continued, turning to Gloria. "Beat them? Remove their balls and eat them for supper? Or bugger them with beer bottles?"

"Before removing the tops, ma'am?" Pak-san asked.

"Yes, before removing the tops, Sergeant."

Kent and Mike looked nervous and sat down on the bed.

"Who are you guys?" asked Todd.

Gloria stood up, walked to the window, surveyed the harbour below and spoke.

"We are a Court of Justice, too. Trying to put right some of the wrongs committed by your predecessors and, now, again by you." She paused and turned towards the men. Even in a bathrobe, and with her hair in a tangle, she cut an impressive figure. "My mother was raped by American officers, and I am the product of that abuse. The daughter of this police superintendent was murdered in Kosovo for not submitting to a US soldier's will. This sergeant's sister was raped and left for dead by marines in Korea. And this maid," she added, pointing to Maya, "was forced to have oral sex with three US naval officers out for a night on the town in Singapore. And now, you try to abuse me."

Gloria turned back to the window and a tear rolled down her cheek. Maya crossed over and put an arm round her friend's shoulder

"Terrorists!" muttered Todd. "Fucking terrorists!"

"No. We do not use the weapons of terror as you do!" Gloria retorted, swinging round to face the men. "You are the terrorists – with your bombs, missiles and napalm."

"What about the beer bottles?" blurted out Kent.

"And cutting off our…" began Mike.

"The Superintendent's bark is louder than her bite," replied Gloria, returning to her seat. "We will not harm you."

Pak-san and Anna began whispering, shaking their heads and pointing at the men.

"Gloria," Pak-san said, "the Superintendent and I feel these brutes deserve more than just the standard re-education programme. Look what they were doing to you!"

"Re-education programme?" Mike and Kent blurted out.

"Surely you want revenge?" pleaded Anna, pulling up a chair next to Gloria and lowering her voice. "You cannot let them get away with trying to rape you! They are criminals who will go unpunished – if we don't take measures."

"I will happily use their balls as practice for my back-kicks!" hissed Pak-san, joining the two women and aiming a near-miss kick at Todd's groin.

Gloria shook her head.

"No violence," she whispered. "We have them at our mercy, and we must show mercy. Remember: re-education is painful, too. What we ask them to do will cause more torment to their souls than any kick-box to their balls or beating of their backsides." She looked up at the men and raised her voice. "I want them to learn the meaning of tenderness. I want them to kiss each other and say they love one another as friends, as fellow men. I want them to caress each other's bodies and discover how to arouse one another through gentleness. I want them to connect to their female sides and bring each other to a peak of excitement with softness and affection."

Mike and Kent appeared confused by this speech, Todd alarmed.

"We're not fucking gay-boys!" he sputtered.

"We're not concerned about your sexuality, and we're not asking you to fuck," replied Gloria. "We're asking you to touch and arouse – with the tip of a finger, or the lick of a tongue – to stroke feel and fondle, not ram disconnected dicks into each other."

"He does that. We don't," chipped in Kent "That's why he's Todd the Butt Man."

"Yeah," chimed in Mike, hoping to join the winning side, too. "He buggers the new boys on the boat, as well as the girls. Don't you, Todd?"

"Shut up, dickhead!" yelled Todd.

"Is that true?" asked Gloria.

"New boys with a fat enough ass and no hair get a two-way split," growled Todd. "Yeah – butt and mouth. They have to learn."

"Learn what?" Maya called out from behind Gloria's chair.

"To do what they're fucking told!" Todd hissed, wrenching at the right handcuff with all his might and glaring at Maya.

"He's a pervert," yelled Kent. "Re-educate him, not us."

"Yeah," added Mike. "It was his idea, bringing you up here. Not ours."

Gloria thought for a moment, then got up and stood in front of Todd.

"Well, Todd. Now, you will learn to do what *you* are told. And Mike and Kent, too," she added, turning to the other men.

"And if we don't?" Todd sneered. "Seeing as you're too soft to hurt us."

Gloria hesitated and turned to Anna.

"We will submit the pictures of you raping Gloria to the real police!" Anna said. "Along with full eyewitness reports from a chambermaid, and the wife of a senior police officer attending a fancy dress party in the adjacent penthouse."

"So, you're not police?" said Kent, gawping at Anna.

"Of course they're not," snarled Todd.

"The penalty for rape in Hong Kong is life imprisonment," continued Anna. "And if you do not follow Gloria's instructions, I will call my husband and he will come with a full team of real policeman to arrest you for the rape of his maid."

"Shit!" hissed Todd.

"And," she concluded, ignoring Todd's expletive, "he already knows that Gloria does escort work to earn extra money for her family back home. I told him."

Gloria glanced up in alarm.

"You told him I did massage only, I hope?"

"Yes," replied Anna, giving Gloria a wink. "He will know this was rape."

Todd hung his head and slumped on the bed.

"What're we going to do?" the other men asked, turning to their leader.

"Do as the goddamn lady says," muttered Todd. "I ain't sitting in a stinking Chink jail for the rest of my life."

"Good," said Gloria. "Let us begin."

Pak-san positioned her video-cam in the corner, framed up the three men and gave a thumbs-up sign. Maya, on a cue from Anna, released the left arm of Kent from the top bedpost leaving only Todd attached at the far end. She then herded the men into a semi-circle, with Kent opposite Todd, and Mike in the middle.

Gloria began her instructions.

"Kent, you are to kiss Todd on the ears and cheeks and lips, and stroke his hair, chest and behind with your free hand. Be smooth and sensuous in your movements. Do not grab and squeeze."

"Jesus!" Todd exclaimed, as Kent leant towards him.

"Mike," Gloria continued, "you are to kneel between your friends and fondle the balls and penis of each of them in turn. Do not rub or grab or pull, but move your hand and fingers with sensitivity, show due respect for the delicate tissue you are touching."

"Fucking hell!" Todd blubbered, as Mike's hand – with his own in enforced pursuit – cupped round his balls and began to stroke them. "Let go of me, you bastard!"

But Mike and Kent ignored the protests and carried out their orders. They weren't going to jail either. Kent's tongue slipped inside Todd's mouth and his free hand fumbled uneasily with the well-muscled left buttock of his fellow officer. Despite himself, Todd's penis swelled and rose in Mike's massaging hand, as did Kent's on the other side.

"Bring them together, Mike," Gloria instructed. "Play the two heads back and forth against each other. Back and forth! Back and forth! Not too hard! Mm!"

And so the programme of re-education followed its usual course, with Gloria, Maya, Anna and Pak-san, taking it in turns to issue instructions to the three men. If any movement was too rough – or the men used too much force, or tried to push the pace – they were reprimanded by the instructor and told to start again. It was Maya who finally made one of them achieve orgasm and, to everyone's surprise, it was Todd. She had asked Kent to take Todd in his mouth, while Mike kissed him on the lips and played with his nipples. To begin with Todd was very aggressive, thrusting violently into Kent's throat and trying to masturbate himself at the same time. But Maya stopped the action and told him to calm down, take a deep breath and let Kent's lips do the work. Kent said his lips were 'kinda sore,' so Maya allowed him and Mike to switch roles. Mike's large buck teeth proved a problem, at first, but eventually his mouth was slipping back and forth along Todd's shaft with an expertise that had even Pak-san applauding. And Kent proved better at caressing Todd's body than Mike – perhaps, because of his free hand and Maya's patient coaching. He was also the best kisser and, thanks to earlier instructions from Anna, knew how to play with Mike's lips, tongue and ears to maximum effect.

As Todd was about to come, Maya ordered Mike to remove the penis from his mouth and let it stand by itself, quivering and glistening in the air. The women watched and waited – the men, too. Then Maya instructed Mike and Kent to kneel either side of the erect member and lick it with their tongues, softly and lovingly. Pak-san moved in with the camera, until all three faces and the perpendicular penis were perfectly in shot.

"Action!" she cried.

The tongues licked, the penis swelled and then its tip erupted, spraying Mike and Kent's faces with the globules of US sperm originally intended for Gloria's anus.

"Smile!" Maya ordered, as the liquid ran down their cheeks. "You too, Todd!"

But Todd was crying, the chief bully bought to book at last.

And that, the team decided, was enough. Gloria felt exhausted, Maya was late for a pole dancing date and Pak-san had an appointment, as a man, with the wife of a Sony executive. It was explained to the three naval officers that, should any of the women in the room be investigated, harmed or persecuted in any way, the contents of the video disc that Pak-san had just shot would be posted on a special website and the entire three-thousand man crew of the aircraft carrier – and selected members of the Pentagon – mailed its contents. In fact, from now on, the men were told, the women would keep tabs on them via US Navy websites – both public and classified – and via a worldwide network of SWAAT women, active at every port of call the US Navy was ever likely to make. Finally, and this was a point stressed by Gloria in particular, the men were to do their utmost to prevent abuse by other men – both on board ship, and ashore.

"If we hear of an incident of rape or abuse in a port where one of your ships has called," she said, standing by the window silhouetted against the city lights, "the secrets of this room will be made public. If we don't, and we feel you are doing your best to promote our programme of re-education, your secrets are safe. Goodnight, gentlemen."

The men, still handcuffed and naked, watched as the women headed to the door.

Kent cleared his throat.

"Ma'am," he said respectfully, holding up his and Mike's wrists.

"Codes to the cuffs will be phoned through in half an hour!" Anna said. "Meanwhile, I suggest you lie on the bed and practice cuddling."

Back in Anna's room, Maya changed into her club clothes and Pak-san put on a pinstriped suit. Gloria lay on the bed while Anna made her an Irish coffee.

"Where did you get the gear, Anna?" Gloria called out.

"The police uniform?"

"Yes."

"Secret!"

"Tell us!" chorused the three women, as Anna brought the coffee across to Gloria and sat on the edge of the bed.

"Too embarrassed," said Anna, turning red.

"We won't tell, will we, girls?" Gloria laughed.

Maya and Pak-san shook their heads.

"Well," began Anna, "my husband likes me to dress up, sometimes."

"Oh, yeah?" cried Pak-san with interest. "As a policeman?"

"Policewoman," said Anna, staring at her lap. "The uniform is from his work."

"And then what?" Pak-san persisted, despite a nudge from Maya.

"He likes me to boss him around and – spank him a bit."

The other women were not sure whether to laugh or look serious.

Then Anna's face broke into a broad grin.

"It's quite fun. We both enjoy it."

Maya hugged Anna. Pak-san was impressed. Gloria sat in silence, a puzzled expression on her face.

"But why was the uniform in our hotel bedroom?" she asked. "You can't have had time to go to Repulse Bay and fetch it – before you came to rescue me?"

"No," said Anna, putting her hand into Gloria's.

"So, why was it here?" Maya repeated, now as curious as the other two.

"Because…" Anna paused and surveyed the women. "Promise to keep this between us?" Three heads nodded. "Because I wanted Gloria to dress up in it tonight and spank me!"

There was a stunned silence, then Pak-san and Maya let out a shriek of triumph, grabbed their bags and did a little jig together to the door.

"At last! At last! Auntie Anna and Sister Gloria. Yes, yes, yes!"

"Just once," said Anna nervously, still waiting for Gloria's response.

"Go on, Gloria," Pak-san pleaded.

Gloria seemed uncertain.

"But we've just taught those boys *not* to be violent…?"

"This is pretend," said Maya, "and with Anna's consent. Those men were forcing you. That's wrong, this is all right. Pak-san and I do it. Don't we, Pak?"

"You do?"

Maya nodded.

"Fine," said Gloria, patting her knee. "Anna? Raise your skirt and bend over!"

Anna hugged Gloria.

Maya took Pak-san's arm and opened the door.

"Have fun!" they called out.

"We will," said Gloria. "And thank you. A successful SWAAT day, after all."

THE RIDERS

I sit in the hayloft above the saddle room. The scent of leather from below blends with the smell of wood smoke wafting in through the open loading door.

It is a late summer afternoon and I am enjoying my last day at home before returning to boarding school. I am just sixteen and have not yet been abroad, smoked a cigarette or kissed a girl. Last term I read a book called *Cold Wind in August*, about a Danish sea scout who is seduced by an older woman. The woman discovers him in the dunes, peels off his trunks and takes him in her hand until he is 'engulfed in a vortex of pleasure.' I was not sure what this meant, but it sounded soft and warm and made me want to go to Denmark. I think about girls closer to home, too, and have a crush on one of the master's wives, but am not worried about being a virgin. At school, I hint I have done more than I have, so other boys respect me. When they talk about shagging girls, I pretend to be bored, and, on a day like today, dream of no more than holding hands. I do not dream further because too much touching disturbs the tenderness. Most girls unsettle me with their knowing stares, and I prefer the company of boys; or, best of all, my own company.

That is why I am here, in the hayloft. I am reading *Wuthering Heights* by Emily Brontë, but have not yet finished the introduction, which goes on and on about the difficulties the children faced after Mrs B passed away. My father died when I was young, but I have a mother and older sister, so can't complain and hope I won't turn to laudanum to solve my problems. My dream is to play in a pop band and compose songs like a new group called the Beatles. Before I heard their music, I was only interested in the classics, but it seems boys in pop groups attract girls without having to make a first move and this appeals to me. I have changed my hairstyle to match John Lennon's, as a first step in my passive seduction strategy, and mother has gone to York this afternoon to buy me a copy of the latest *Fab Magazine* – an edition devoted entirely to the Beatles.

In fact, there is no one at home today apart from me: mother in York, Cook on a day off and sister Clare at the village gymkhana. Clare lives for riding and goes for long 'hacks' with a village girl called Stella. Stella scares me and I cannot imagine what she and my sister have in common – apart from horses.

We have three, but I have never taken to riding. When I was small, mother took me to 'meets' of the local hunt and showed me off to the county set. We squeezed between steaming flanks and sweaty withers with, far above, men and women in boots, breeches and black hats, brandishing whips and sipping sherry. Scary. Particularly the women, who grinned down at me with red lips and tickled my nose with their crops, or, if I came too near to the hind legs of their mounts, shouted "Get away, you wretched little boy!" Some horses had red ribbons round their tails, a sign they might kick. Their owners – usually veiled women in long black skirts riding side saddle – were the fiercest of all.

My thoughts are interrupted by the sound of horses' hooves. I put down my book and listen. The clip-clop of metal on tarmac approaches, coming up the back lane beneath the hayloft door. Could it be my sister returning? I look at my watch. It is already half past five. I have been daydreaming and the afternoon has slipped away. I hear the horses turn into our yard and halt outside the saddle room. I recognize my sister Clare's voice and the Yorkshire twang of Stella.

Damn! I do not want to be disturbed, and do not want to meet Stella and be forced to make polite conversation. I debate jumping out of the hay-loading door, but it is a fair drop and I decide to stay put. No reason for either of the girls to come up to the loft, and once they have removed their saddles and rubbed down the horses, they will head to the house. Well, Clare will – Stella, I hope, will go home. I do not fancy having Stella Duffin, from the village council estate, as a dinner guest on my last night at home.

I hear them dismount and walk their horses into the two single stables. There is a jangling of stirrups as saddles are removed and then silence, interspersed with the occasional neigh from one or other of the horses as the girls rub them down. Then, one by one, I hear the stable doors close and the saddles – again with a jangling of stirrups – being carried into the saddle room below me. The girls are chatting, though I cannot hear what they say, and I wait with bated breath for them to store away their kit and leave.

But now there is silence, followed, after a while, by giggling. I shake my head in frustration. Then I freeze. Someone is climbing up the ladder to the loft. I grab my book and hide behind some bales of hay. Through a gap I see the trap door open upwards. Clare – in white blouse, Pony Club tie, breeches and boots – emerges, followed by Stella in identical clothes and carrying a Brownie 127 camera and a riding switch. Clare's blonde hair is bunched in a bun at the back of her head and she has a rosette pinned to her blouse – Stella, whose hair is jet-black and tied in a ponytail, is laughing and tapping Claire on the bottom with the switch to make her hurry up.

What are they doing here? Looking for me? I crouch down and hold my breath.

I watch as Stella takes Clare in her arms and kisses her on the mouth. Clare does not protest, but puts her arms around Stella's waist and holds her tight. I feel excitement mount in my body and keep still. Then a gust of wind from the open loading door disturbs chaff on the loft floor. The dust floats up a shaft of sunlight and into my nose. My body prepares to reject it. Damn again! I try to avert the approaching sneeze, but cannot. It explodes into the silence of the barn.

The girls stop kissing. I sneeze again, and then a third time and watch in dismay as Stella strides across the floor, pulls away the bales of hay and stares down at me.

"Little brother hiding in loft?" she says in her broad Yorkshire accent. "Come over here, Clare. Look what cat dragged in."

Clare comes over red-faced and cross.

"What are you doing here, Robert?" she demands.

"Minding my own business," I reply, brushing hay from my white Aertex shirt and khaki shorts.

"Well, go and mind your business somewhere else," she says "Stella and I…"

She pauses.

"Have some business of your own?" I ask. "So I saw."

"Don't tell Mother!" Clare shouts, putting her hands on her hips.

Stella watches us, a smirk on her face. Then, tucking the switch under her arm, she lifts the Brownie camera to her eye and clicks.

"Stella!" Clare shouts. "What are you doing?"

"Taking pictures," Stella replies, as she winds on to take a second snap.

"Well, don't," Clare says in her poshest, bossiest voice. "Go and soap the saddles. I'll deal with Robert."

Stella scowls, brandishing the camera at Clare.

"What about photos?"

"Not now. Some other time."

"Scared he'll tell?" sneers Stella, heading for the trap door. "He'd enjoy it."

"Stella!" Clare shouts again, her face turning red. "Go and soap the saddles."

"Yes, madam!"

Stella disappears down the ladder. Clare sits on a bale of hay and stares at me.

"You won't tell, will you, Robert?"

Her voice is softer now. I shake my head.

"I've seen girls kiss before," I say, resorting to the bluff technique used at school.

"Have you? You're not shocked?"

I shake my head and pat Clare on the shoulder. She hugs me and stands up.

"Let's go. I promised Mum I'd start the dinner."

"Is…" I point to the saddle room below, "…coming?"

"She was. I'll ask her to go home, now. Your last night of hols, isn't it?"

I nod.

The saddle-room door below slams and we both laugh. Stella has departed – in a huff no doubt. We cross to the trap door and Clare starts to descend.

"Clare?" I ask, before she disappears. "What were the pictures Stella mentioned?"

"Nothing," Clare replies. "Just snaps to celebrate my win at the gymkhana."

"I'd keep clear of Stella, if I were you."

"Why?" Clare asks, resting her elbows on the loft floor. "Don't you like her?"

"She's a village girl and…"

"Snob!" Clare laughs. "I suppose you think I should 'mix with my own sort?'"

I shrug my shoulders.

"You may be right," Clare adds, as an afterthought. "She is a bit strange."

Clare disappears through the trap door. I follow her, easing my feet on to the top rung of the ladder as those of my sister reach the tiled floor below. Then I hear a gasp.

"Stella!"

When I descend, I find Stella leaning against the door to the stable yard, brandishing a key in one hand and her switch in the other. It is too dark to discern the expression on her face, as I have closed the trap door and there is only a single, sixty-watt light bulb illuminating the windowless room.

I look for Clare and see that she has retreated to a saddle horse behind the ladder.

"We thought you'd gone," Clare stutters, her face white beneath the naked bulb.

I join my sister and put an arm around her shoulder. We both stare at Stella.

"'Strange village girl?' Not good enough to come to dinner?" she says.

"Just silly talk," Clare replies, trying to calm her friend.

The switch hisses through the air and hits the side of Stella's riding boot.

"Stella!" Clare resorts to her imperious tone. "Go. We'll talk about this later."

"Someone to 'keep clear of?'" Stella mutters, advancing towards me.

I am about to speak, but Clare holds a finger to her mouth and steps forward.

"What do you want, Stella?"

"Fun," retorts Stella. "Like you and I were planning, 'til brother poked his nose in."

Clare turns to me.

"Run along, Robert. Then Stella can take her photos."

I shrug my shoulders and head for the door. Let the girls sort things out. But the door is locked and when I hold out my hand for the key, Stella laughs.

"Want some fun with you and all."

I raise my eyebrows and approach Stella to take the key. Clare holds up a hand.

"Stella," she says, her voice soft and reasonable. "It's Robert's last day at home. He doesn't want to be locked up in a dark room with us. Give him the key."

Stella shakes her head. This time both my sister and I stride towards her, but she stands her ground and holds up the camera round her neck.

"Bet your mother'd like to see photos," she says. "Wouldn't she, Clare?"

Clare stares in horror at her friend.

"You wouldn't."

"I would. And post 'em on the church board. Unless you two do just what I say."

I glance at Clare. She is shaking. I sit her down on a stool by the saddle horse.

"What's she talking about?" I ask.

"She took some photos, last week."

"What of?"

"Me and her. In a field."

"Doing what?" I ask

Clare buries her face in her hands.

"Dirty things," Stella grins. "Things little school boys don't know about."

"Is this true?" I say to Clare.

Clare nods, face still in her hands.

"She works Saturdays at the chemists in Malton. Develops them herself."

I approach Stella. Our mother is a regular churchgoer. Any scandal would not only upset her, but also have an adverse effect on her health. She has a weak heart and the doctor told us to make sure she avoids stressful situations.

"Listen to me," I begin, "you show any pictures to Mrs Mason and I'll…"

"You'll do what, little boy?" she sneers. "Come and beat me up? I've three brothers, you know, and they don't like boarding school boys like you. Not one bit they don't. They'd beat you up and bugger you to boot, I wouldn't mind."

Brothers apart, Stella is a tall girl and well-built from working in the fields. I am not sure I could take her on and win. Also, she has a switch in her hand. I make a grab for the key, but she whisks it behind her back and walks across to my sister.

"Well?" she demands, playing the switch through Clare's hair. "Photos or fun?"

Clare glances up at her friend and then at me.

"What do you want us to do?" she asks.

"You can soap saddles for a start. And he can take his shirt and shorts off. Not seen brother's body, have I?"

Clare gets up, but this time goes over to Stella and falls on her knees.

"Please, Stella. Please. Do what you like with me. But leave him out of it."

Stella glances down at Clare and again ruffles the blonde hair with her switch.

"It's him, or photos on church board. Sister and brother, or no deal."

I think fast. Even if the photographs are just of Clare kissing Stella, I do not want my mother to see them – either at home or on the church board. Nor do I want my sister shamed. She is young and healthy and could withstand the shock, but it is an old-fashioned and upright community, and if she were associated with Stella in an unsavoury way, people would cease to respect and admire her as they do now. And there is myself to think of, too.

Although I go to boarding school, it is only twelve miles away, at Ampleforth, and news of the scandal might well reach members of staff and even some of the boys as well. I do not know what Stella has in store for us, but anything played out in the secrecy of our saddle room is better than compromising pictures of my sister being published. And, to be honest, I am curious. If I were by myself with Stella, it would be less embarrassing and a story to tell the other boys. But she wants us both, so here goes.

"I don't mind," I say, removing shirt and shorts and stripping down to my Y-fronts. "People see me on the beach like this, don't they?"

"That's better," says Stella, throwing me a sponge from a drawer in the base of the saddle horse. "And here's one for you, sis."

She tosses a sponge at my sister and indicates two saddles on the saddle horse. This waist-high wooden dummy dominates the room and reminds me of childhood cowboy games with Clare. I take the tin of saddle soap from a shelf by the door, balance it on the end of the horse and dip my sponge into the yellow, translucent paste. I begin to soap the darker of the two saddles. Clare, still glancing at Stella and mouthing 'Sorry' at me, takes a second sponge and starts on the lighter saddle.

Stella walks back and forth behind us, saying nothing. After a while, she comes and leans against the end of the saddle horse nearest to me.

"You ever been with a girl?" she asks.

I am unprepared for the question and blush. That is enough answer for her.

"Thought not – little virgin brother. Stuck it up a boy's bum though, have you?"

I shake my head, feeling the blush spread over my bare chest.

"One of ones t'others bugger?" she insists. "Prefects' bum boy? Read about them."

"Certainly not!" I burst out in indignation.

"'Certainly not,'" she says, imitating my posh voice. "Thought you were all queer at private schools. No girls, so you bugger one another."

She returns to pacing. I ignore her, and concentrate on soaping. It's true, boys do climb into each other's beds at night, but I'm not sure what they do and have never dared to take part. I find one or two of the younger boys attractive – especially when dressed up as women in the school plays – but the older boys are too hairy and rough for me.

Stella stops pacing and leans against the saddle horse near my sister.

"Ever seen a full-grown girl naked?" she says, still talking to me.

I shake my head.

"Not even your sister?"

I shake my head again and concentrate on the harder leather of the girth strap. Suddenly Stella pushes Clare to the floor.

"On your hands and knees, sis. Let bro see what a nice bum you've got."

I feel anger mounting, but remember the photographs.

"You all right, Clare?"

Clare nods and remains on all fours.

"No talking!" snaps Stella. "Unless I say so. Understood?"

We both nod.

"Sit on that stool, Robert. And watch."

I sit on a stool, positioned directly behind Clare's kneeling legs. I watch as Stella lowers my sister's breeches to knee level. Her round behind, in blue cotton underwear, arouses me despite myself. I avert my gaze and stare at the floor. Stella notices.

"Embarrassed? Didn't know your sister had a bum like that, did you? Go on, pull her knickers down," she goads.

I shake my head.

"I said pull her knickers down," Stella repeats, standing over me with the switch.

I slip off the stool and, without looking, take hold of my sister's underpants and pull them down.

"That's better," says Stella, settling on the stool behind me. "Now, have a feel."

I shake my head. She whips me across the buttocks with her switch. I wince.

"Do as she says, Rob," Clare calls out. "I'll be all right."

I kneel behind my sister, reach out my hands and, for the first time, feel the soft, firm flesh of my sister's behind, of any woman's behind.

I stroke it, and stroke it again – and again feel aroused. Stella sees my excitement and yanks down my Y-fronts.

"You like her, so fuck her. Go on! Fuck her, little brother," she yells. "Go on! Fuck your big sister. Stick it up her."

I hesitate, out of shock at being naked in front of two women, and because I have no idea what I am meant to do.

"I said fuck her," she shouts again, hitting my bare buttocks with her switch.

"What do you mean?" I stutter.

Stella roars with laughter, and coming round in front of me, grabs my penis and starts trying to push it between my sister's legs.

"You really are a virgin, aren't you? It's like mating a stallion with mare for first time. Bloody hell. Get bugger in hole. Not there!"

As it dawns on me what she is trying to do, I pull away from Stella's grasp.

"This is going too far," I shout. "You're mad!"

"Why?" Stella retorts, momentarily shocked by my protest.

"Making me do that, with my sister." I say, crouching on the stool, hands between my legs.

"Village folk do it all the time," retorts Stella. "That's why we're mad."

I start to sob. Stella taps Clare on the behind with her switch.

"Bro's blubbing. Give him a cuddle."

With breeches and underpants trailing round her ankles, Clare crawls across the floor and puts an arm over my shoulder. I can see she has been crying, too.

"I've not finished yet," Stella warns. "We'll call this a tea break."

I am comforted by the gentle touch of my sister and want to put my arms around her. But then she will see me naked and I do not want that. So I sit crouched, hands between my legs, while she hugs me. I do not understand why Stella is being so cruel. Is it because we are rich and she is not? Is it because she enjoys seeing us naked? Enjoys humiliating us? Is this what older people do? And what about me? A woman just grabbed my penis for the first time and it went limp? Does this mean I do not like women? That I am not normal? Thoughts whirl round my head and become too much. I start to cry again.

"Sorry, Clare," I sob. "I'm not being much help."

"Don't worry," Clare whispers. "She'll get bored. Just do as she says."

"Even that?"

"No, not that," my sister says. "You were right not to do that."

A click and a flash and, looking up, I see Stella with her Brownie.

"Now Mum'll see both her kiddies," she laughs. "So better do what I say."

"Stella…" Clare begins, but then shakes her head. "Oh, get on with it."

"Thank you, madam," Stella replies.

She puts down the camera, approaches Clare, and kisses her on the mouth while rubbing her between the legs. She then removes my sister's tie, blouse and brassiere and tells her to stand in front of me, in the light. Clare still has her boots on, with her breeches and underpants hanging round her calves and ankles. She has to shuffle across the floor to reach the illuminated area beneath the light bulb. Stella takes my head in her hands and lifts it up, so that I am staring at my sister's body. I have never seen a naked woman in the flesh before. In the nudist magazines that boys circulate at school, the part around the groin is always airbrushed out, so the hair surprises me. And the roundness of the body, which is smooth and soft and luscious looking, and I wish it were not my sister's.

"Nice tits," Stella says, moving behind Clare to lift up her breasts. "Want a suck?"

My sister grimaces, but nods at me. I move forward, hands over groin, bend down and put my lips to Clare's nipple. When I suck, it goes hard. I feel aroused, and even more so when Clare puts her hand around my neck and strokes it. I hear Stella behind me, her riding boots clicking on the tiled floor.

"And now t'other one," she orders.

I move my mouth to the right nipple, and suck. Clare fondles my ears and strokes my hair, and I wonder whether what we are doing is wrong if it feels so nice.

Then a hand pushes between my legs, grabs my balls and squeezes. The combination of pain below and pleasure above is strange, but, to my surprise, increases the excitement. I suck, Clare strokes, Stella squeezes.

I suck, Stella squeezes, Clare strokes. Clare strokes, Stella squeezes, I suck. I release my hands from their position over my groin and slide them around the smooth hips of my sister until they are holding her behind. I squeeze and stroke, as well as being squeezed and stroked; my fingers running up and down the gap between her buttocks, my body getting harder all the time. I feel myself moving closer to my sister, I hear my sister sigh in an unusual way. I do not understand what is happening; my body is taking control of my mind.

"Between her legs," snaps Stella. "On all fours and lick sister."

I hesitate, but Clare gently pushes my head down. I kneel, ignoring the cold of the tiles, and see the triangle of hair in front of me. It tickles my nose, but the aroma draws me on. It is unlike anything I have smelt; a sweet sweaty scent, arousing me further and combining with the sensations of touch and sight in an imperceptible, indivisible way.

"Hold it open, Clare," Stella commands, and then I feel her climb onto my back and sit astride me like a horse.

Clare's fingers open pink lips hidden within the blonde curly hair. Her free hand guides my mouth towards a button of flesh exposed at the top of the lips. I hesitate. I am about to lick a girl's private parts and that girl is my sister. I feel excited but scared, as if I am about to taste forbidden fruit. Is this the vortex? Is this what adults do? Is this sex?

"Lick her!" Stella yells from above, and I feel her switch sting my behind.

My tongue touches the glistening button of flesh. The taste is sweet and salty, and the wetness that I lick has the consistency of honey. My sister shudders and caresses my ears and hair. Am I hurting her? Is that why she shakes? Stella notices my hesitation and hits me twice, like a horse reluctant to go to water. I lick again and again and my sister's sighs grow in intensity, her hands holding my head more firmly in place while still continuing their caressing. If I were hurting her, she would push me away. So I lick, and the more I lick, the more her honey seems to flow. Above me, I feel Stella lean forward.

"Big sister likes baby brother's mouth," she hisses next to my ear. "And, while you do that, I'm going to squeeze sister's nipples and kiss sister's lips. So don't stop."

Stella hits me with the switch to reinforce her words. I hear my sister gasp, followed by the sound of kissing. I feel saliva drop on to the back of my neck. I increase the pace of my licking and start to suck the honey off the wet pink lips and button, drawing the soft flesh in and out of my mouth as I do so. Stella is rotating her own groin into my back and starting to grunt herself, and the more she grunts the more she hits me with the switch. But my sister's wetness and the softness of her hands on my head remove the pain or convert the pain into a sting of pleasure, and, with each cut of the switch, I feel myself grow between the legs until my whole body threatens to explode.

But my sister explodes first with a cry of agony. I withdraw my mouth and look up. All I can see is Stella's right hand clamped to Clare's erect, left nipple.

"Is she all right?" I gasp. "What have you done to her?"

"What have I done?" scoffs Stella. "Nowt — but you 'ave. You given her a bleedin' thingamajig. Dirty boy making big sister come in his mouth. Yuk!"

She climbs off my back. I stand up and take Clare in my arms. I am concerned that something bad has happened and do not understand what Stella has just said.

But my penis is still erect and pushes in between my sister's legs. I feel embarrassed and Clare does too. She removes my arms and edges away from me.

"I'm all right," she says, but her cheeks and breasts are red and flushed.

"Are you sure?" I say.

"Yes," she hisses. "Just leave me alone."

She hobbles off, breeches and underpants round her ankles, and huddles on the stool. I am left standing alone beneath the naked light bulb, not sure what to do. Despite the situation, my penis remains erect. I cover it, but Stella approaches, pulls my hands away and flicks at the hardened flesh with the end of her switch. I wince.

"What we gonna do about that, then?"

I shake my head.

"A stuck-up little bugger like its owner, isn't it?" she continues, flicking the penis again so that it wobbles from side to side. "Big one though."

She puts her thumb and forefinger round her chin and stares at my groin.

"Needs emptying, that one does," she says. "Now, what's best way to make a stuck-up boarding-school prick shoot its load?"

She walks round me, chin still resting in her hand, switch tucked under her arm. She stops behind me, takes a step forward and parts my buttocks.

"Squeeze it out from back end, I'd say. Like toothpaste."

She gives my balls a flick with the switch and walks to a fodder bin by the door. She lifts the lid, rummages inside and pulls out a parsnip.

"Big enough, lad?" she grins, holding it up.

I do not know what she is talking about and, as with older boys at school, my only tactic is to stay silent. But Clare looks up in alarm.

"Don't do that, Stella!" she pleads.

"Nowt wrong with a bit of buggery," replies Stella, knocking away a clump of earth from the parsnip's tip. "Do it all the time where he goes to school. Don't they?"

I shrug my shoulders again, wishing my penis would shrink. It seems to be the sole centre of Stella's attention.

"Up on the saddle horse!" she orders.

"What do you mean?" I ask

"Get on the saddle at far end of horse and pretend you're a jockey."

I survey the horse and the two half-soaped saddles. They are both facing in the same direction, so I walk to the one nearest Clare's stool and swing my leg over the top until I am sitting astride the horse. The damp leather feels cool against my balls and legs.

"Now put your feet in stirrups," Stella directs, "and stick your bum in air!"

The stirrups are high and once my feet are in them, my knees are forced upwards and outwards. My behind is still resting on the saddle and my penis is sticking straight up in the air. I feel a fool and uncomfortable. I watch as Stella pulls the legs of her breeches out of the top of her boots and unzips the side fasteners. She slips them down over her boots and pulls them off one by one. Watching makes me more excited and I turn away.

"Keep looking," she calls. "Don't want Willy wilting, do we?"

I watch as she takes off her tie and blouse and stands staring at me in her boots, bra and underpants.

"Like it?" she asks.

I nod.

"More than big sister?"

I nod again.

"Good."

She picks up the parsnip and approaches the saddle horse. It comes up to her waist, and she stands for a moment staring down at my penis. Then she dips the end of the parsnip in the open tin of saddle soap and waves it under my nose.

"Know where that's going?" she grins.

I shake my head.

"You soon will."

She climbs onto the saddle behind me. I cannot see her, but, at last, realise what she plans to do. I want her to stop, but then think of the pictures and my mother's face.

"If I let you do this," I ask, "will you let us go?"

"Maybe. If toothpaste comes out all right."

"And give us the photographs back? All of them?"

"Aye, lad! Deal's a deal. You ready?"

I nod. Part of me is apprehensive, but part of me is excited – by the rough tone of Stella's voice, by her earthy smell and her half-naked body behind me.

"Clare," she calls. "Come and hold your brother's hand. He might cry."

Clare, still trailing her breeches, shuffles to the end of the saddle horse.

"Don't hurt him," she says.

"I'll do me best," laughs Clare, and taps me on the shoulder. "Stand up in stirrups and lean forward, lad. Like a jockey."

I do as she asks, until my head is almost touching the end of the saddle horse and my behind is stuck in the air. Clare takes my hand, squeezes it and strokes my hair.

"Try and relax," she whispers. "It won't hurt so much."

I nod and wince as the tip of the parsnip touches the rim of my anus.

"Oh, no!" hisses Clare.

"What is it?" I ask.

"Never mind."

"Tell me," I whisper.

"She's going to touch herself as she does it. She's put a hand in her pants."

"What do you mean?"

"Never mind. Just hold tight. It may get rough."

I close my eyes as the tip of the parsnip pushes into my anus. It is like I am being invaded. It feels wrong, wrong and unnatural, but also arousing – painful and arousing at the same time. I open my eyes and know there are tears forming in them. I smile at my sister and she wipes the Beatle fringe back off my forehead.

"Clare," I whisper.

"Yes, Robert?"

"Will you kiss me?"

"Properly?" she says, a mixture of shock and excitement in her voice.

"Like you did with Stella," I say. "When I was hiding."

I wince as the parsnip is driven up inside me, forcing tears from my eyes. Clare licks the tears away, moves her mouth to mine and pushes her tongue between my lips. I have never tasted anything so sweet, my whole body is filled with warmth and tenderness and a yearning to belong.

And, from then on, each time Stella drives the parsnip in, my sister kisses me and strokes my hair and ears and neck. I am in heaven and hell at once, and sense that one cannot exist without the other. The urgent pushing and withdrawing behind – the soft lips in front; the hardening and throbbing of my penis – the gentle mixing of my lips with Clare's; soft and hard, pain and pleasure, agony and consolation. This is my initiation into the world of grown-ups, my Adam's apple, the innocence of childhood expelled from my body by a parsnip and a sister's kiss. I groan and Stella groans, and her thrusting gets harder and more brutal, and the kisses of Clare become more tender and wetter and sweeter – I am going to explode, I am going to explode, I am...

The sound of a key turning in the door – someone has found the spare that sits in a drainpipe by the stables. Someone is coming in.

We freeze. I can feel Clare's mouth freeze on mine, I can feel Stella's hand freeze with the parsnip half inserted, I can feel my whole body freeze – right on the point of explosion – freeze as hard and cold as ice.

"Hello?" a voice calls, as the door opens. "Anyone home?"

It is mother. Out of the corner of my eye, I see a copy of *Fab Magazine* in her hand. On the cover is a picture of John Lennon.

Then hand and picture disappear from view, and I hear a body hit the floor.